BADGER ISLAND

With a grunt that was audible only to those behind him, Krag ran forward with all the speed that his tired muscles could muster, heading directly for the nearest point where the wood joined the fields.

"Hey, look! Over there! There's some of 'em got out!"

Krag did not understand the words but he knew that they had been seen. The diggers hastily threw down their spades, grabbed for their shotguns. Three deafening explosions crashed out, the reports echoing and re-echoing across the surrounding countryside. Pellets, leaden death, whistled all around the fleeing badgers. Krag felt a stinging pain in his rump, another on his broad back close to the snare.

BADGER ISLAND

Jonathan Guy

RED FOX

For Rowan, Tara
Gavin and Angus

A Red Fox Book

Published by Random House Children's Books
20 Vauxhall Bridge Road, London SW1V 2SA

A division of Random House UK Ltd

London Melbourne Sydney Auckland
Johannesburg and agencies throughout the world

© Jonathan Guy 1993

First published by Julia MacRae Books 1993

Red Fox edition 1994

1 3 5 7 9 10 8 6 4 2

Printed and bound in Great Britain by
Cox & Wyman Ltd, Reading, Berkshire

RANDOM HOUSE UK Limited Reg. No. 954009

ISBN 0 09 918951 8

Contents

Part One

SPRING

Chapter One

There had been badgers in Hopwas Wood for as long as the inhabitants of the small village could remember. The huge sett amidst the gnarled and twisted oak and beech trees had been there when the oldest of them were children, and their fathers and grandfathers before them had spoken of it, too. Little had changed over the years. Each Spring fresh excavations in the extensive clearing were proof enough for any who cared to go and see for themselves that the animals were preparing for yet another cycle. Winter bedding, moss, leaves and bracken had been removed, a fresh supply replacing the old in readiness for the coming breeding season. In a few weeks another generation of badgers would be born to succeed the existing ones when their time came. For these creatures, life went on much the same, year in, year out.

Seldom were the badgers seen by humans, with the exception of old Jenkins, the gamekeeper, for they were nocturnal creatures, sleeping by day and foraging for food by night. Jenkins glimpsed them from time to time when he roamed his preserves on moonlit nights, but he did not trouble them for they did little harm to his hand-reared pheasants. Occasionally, a badger was caught in one of the snares which he set for Rus, the dog-fox, and Tosca, the vixen. When that happened, this guardian of the fields and coverts freed the captured badger, taking care to inflict as little pain as possible in the process. He threw his coat over the struggling animal's head, and pinned it to the ground with the cleft of a forked stick whilst he cut the wire. Then he stood back, watched the badger scuttle to freedom, surprised at the unexpected reprieve which it had been granted. Jenkins regretted that he had to set his wires in the wood, but he had no alternative for it was also inhabited by the foxes which preyed on his pheasant poults. He admired Rus, but in a different way. Rus was a noble and cunning foe, a ruthless killer so much in contrast to the badger, preying on the birdlife and smaller animals of the countryside. Jenkins tried to maintain a balance of wildlife, to protect and control but not to exterminate any species. There would have been none sadder than Jenkins had Rus and Tosca completely disappeared from these woodlands.

Krag, the badger leader, was getting on in years, not *really* old but past the prime of his life. He had realized this during the recent Winter when, for weeks on end, he had lain in the deepest chamber of the big sett along with Jetta, his mate, and the rest of the colony. After darkness had fallen, they emerged above ground to forage through the dead undergrowth in search of edible roots, mice, voles and perhaps a hibernating hedgehog if they were lucky.

Now, with the coming of Spring, Krag basked in the warm sunshine on the rocky ledge above the sett whilst the rest of them remained below ground as was their custom. Krag preferred this daytime solitude of late, a combination of wariness, in case of the intrusion of an enemy, and a desire to remain aloof from his companions. The biting cold winter wind had been replaced by a gentle, warm breeze. Sheep bleated in the surrounding fields. One or two of the ewes already had lambs, born prematurely during the driving

4

blizzards and somehow surviving the drifting snow, the prowling Rus and the watchful eye of Raol, the carrion crow, who sensed when a mother was unable to protect her offspring and glided down to his prey, his razor sharp beak a weapon of cruel, instant death.

For Krag, life was like a herd of lazy cattle moving slowly across a distant skyline. He knew and accepted the laws decreed by Nature. When the leaves fell again the badgers would demand a new leader, one who was more agile, more alert. There would be several contenders amongst the young boars. Baal was the most aggressive although he lacked the wisdom and experience of Krag. Age-old badger lore demanded that the issue be settled by a fight to the death, a challenge made by a younger animal and taken up by the older one. At the moment, though, a strong friendship existed between the two of them. Krag would have preferred to concede his position amicably and remain in the sett to advise Baal on the ways of Man and beast, but he knew only too well that it could not happen that way. When the days shortened, and the hoar frosts returned, then Baal would forget their relationship. There was no other way. Baal would not wait for another Spring.

Krag understood most of the wildlife which existed around him, not only in Hopwas Wood but in the neighbouring woodlands as well. He also knew a little about the ways of Man. Around Krag's body, the coarse fur having long grown over it, the wire noose of a fox snare bit into his flesh. Three winters past he had become caught in it during a foray into Swinfen Wood across the main road towards the city. It had been a moonless night and he had followed a track through a gap in a straggling hawthorn hedge, the still atmosphere alive with the scent of Rus, a sour odour. But Rus had been wiser, somehow sensing the snare and turning back. Krag had scuttled on, straight into the noose. The wire had slipped from its setting, the noose widening, and it had run halfway down his body before it had tightened and held him.

He had struggled for a time, pulling in a desperate attempt to snap the strong wire but his panic only made it cut deeper into his skin. In the end he had flopped down, resigned himself to his fate. Man, the only enemy of the badgers, had finally outwitted him.

The long night passed, and just after dawn on a cold, grey morning, he heard human footsteps approaching. He pulled back as far as the wire would allow, stood at bay, fearful yet defiant. He determined that, if possible, his jaws would leave their mark on his enemy before he was killed.

He recognized Jenkins; the large floppy hat, the bulky jacket and baggy plus-fours, beneath his arm the stick which made a loud bang and heralded death to the creatures of the wild. A labrador dog ran forward eagerly, stopped, its hackles raised. It growled, backed away. Krag scented its fear and it pleased him. He stood there, watching and waiting.

"Sorry, old feller," there was a gruff sympathy in the old gamekeeper's voice. "Come away, Sam, or you'll get bitten for sure and you can't blame Brock if he does get his teeth into you. Now, hang on a minute while I cut a stick."

Krag did not understand the other's words but he sensed the kindliness in them. All the same, he did not trust humans. If either Man or dog came close enough, he would launch himself at them because that was the law of survival. Jenkins laid his gun down, walked over to an ash tree and began hacking at a branch with his knife. The stout bough was fashioned into a forked stick within minutes.

Jenkins came back, took off his jacket, and stood looking at Krag apprehensively. "Now, we'll soon have you out of there, Brock!"

Krag lunged forward, grunting, his powerful jaws wide. The wire checked him when he was only inches from the man's legs, and bowled him over. Suddenly, a suffocating blackness enveloped the old badger, blotting out the greyness of the dawn. Something fastened behind his neck, pinning him helplessly to the ground. His struggles were to no avail. A heavy boot pressed down on him, held him still. That was when he gave up, and waited for death.

Human fingers probed the coarse hair, located the wire noose. More pain followed; a burning sensation that encircled the middle of his body as Jenkins pulled and twisted.

"Swivel's twisted, I'll have to cut you free."

There was a brief pause whilst Krag's captor fumbled in the pockets of his large trousers, and found a pair of wire-cutters. Krag lay immobile, not understanding, not caring. He heard and felt the snip; then the coat was removed from his head, the sudden dawn light causing him to blink. It was some seconds before he realized that he was free. He stood there bewildered, staring at the gamekeeper who had stepped back and picked up his gun, fearing a sudden attack from those powerful jaws.

"Off you go, then, and don't come back."

Krag ran off with surprising agility. It took him a very short time to complete the distance back to Hopwas Wood where he at once retired to his own quarters, not wishing the other badgers to know that he had been foolish enough to blunder into a snare. Except Jetta, his mate. Her fur was much darker in colour than the average badger, a fine sow who had come from the sett in Swinfen Wood and stayed with him, had been at his side when he was but a young boar on the badger council.

Now she licked his wound for him and discovered that the wire noose was still there, cutting into his skin. Jenkins, whose eyesight was beginning to fail, had severed the snare *above* the swivel. The noose would remain on Krag for the rest of his days.

The days passed, and now there was a sweetness about

7

the breeze as Krag lay and basked in the sunshine on the rocky shelf above the big sett. Winter was truly over at last, and the old badger sensed the changes that were coming with Spring, more than just the beginning of a new cycle. The others would not tolerate an ageing leader for much longer, they were already becoming restless, and he was powerless to alter the laws of the wild.

Towards the end of January, Jenkins had passed away peacefully and now lay in the village churchyard. A new gamekeeper had been appointed, and had Krag known who that man was he would, in all probability, have led the badgers to a place of greater safety whilst he still occupied the role of leader. In these remote woodland places humans were recognized by the creatures of the wild, mostly by sight, occasionally by scent. Davies, the farmer, was always recognizable by his long brown smock and his unhurried climb up to the higher slopes in search of a missing ewe. The stick which he carried never barked instant death to the rabbits or hares which bounded up at his feet. Jones, the shepherd from over the other side of the hill, seldom seen in these parts, harmed none either. But Reuben . . .

Reuben was known to all species of fur and feather, and they feared him. Young and agile, he was capable of penetrating the most formidable slopes and dense thickets, his long greasy hair straggling in the wind, his jacket of mottled green and brown with trousers to match that often rendered him invisible in the undergrowth, never without his gun nor the pack of yapping, hunting terriers at his heels. The inhabitants of the wood knew Warrior, too, the killer terrier, scarred after many battles with badgers and foxes below ground, always scenting. Always hunting.

But, as Krag's instincts had already warned him, there were going to be changes. Gamekeepers were not easily come by, and the shooting syndicate in the city, who relied upon these woodlands for their weekend sport during the winter months, cared little for the character of the man whom they employed to look after their pheasants. They decided that a poacher, a fellow who understood the ways of the wild and suddenly found himself in a position of responsibility, could well be their best choice. So, within a week of Jenkins' funeral, Reuben rose from the dubious role of poacher to the entrusted position of gamekeeper; the land which he had once roamed for nefarious reasons, he could now patrol with authority. He accepted the position with relish, and at once informed his former cronies. Now they had the freedom of the countryside, and they remembered the badger sett in Hopwas Wood.

Chapter Two

*K*rag stirred, his drowsiness disappearing instantly with the harsh screeching of the finely plumaged jay in the deep woods. A warning. Danger. Perhaps there was a sparrow-hawk in the vicinity in which case it would not worry the badgers. Only the songbirds and woodpigeons would need to seek shelter, for this daytime cousin of the nocturnal owl was a ruthless predator.

The jay continued to shriek incessantly. Krag tensed, eased himself up. He understood the warning now, there was no mistaking it.

Man. Man. Run. Hide.

Then he heard the distant baying, the drumming of hooves. A horn.

The Hunt!

The red-coated hunstmen who rode in the wake of a pack of streaming hounds did not worry Krag unduly. Neither men nor dogs concerned themselves with badgers, they were only interested in foxes, Rus and Tosca. This would be the last hunt of the season, they would not return again until after the leaves had fallen. Krag listened, followed the progress of the Hunt, determining distance and direction by sound alone because of his natural short-sightedness.

They were drawing Hopwas Wood, the hounds well ahead of their masters on the steep incline that led up from the Lady Walk. Slowly, Krag moved back towards the sett. It would be unwise to remain in the open. Just a short time below ground and then it would be safe to emerge again.

He experienced a sadness towards Rus and Tosca. The badger colony tolerated the foxes, a kind of mutual respect existing between the two species. During the winter months, when the snow lay deep on the wooded hillsides, Rus and his mate occupied the upper gallery of the big sett whilst the badgers lived in the deepest chamber. The foxes were not welcome tenants for they had not the clean habits of their landlords and their rank smell often drifted down into the lower regions when the wind blew from the north. Krag always turned the foxes out once Spring arrived and it was time for the badgers to renovate their home. Usually the fox smell was gone within a couple of days of their departure. He wondered if the badger who succeeded him as leader would show such tolerance towards a fellow creature of the woods.

Krag hurried along the well-used track which led to the sett. Rus and Tosca must go *now*! He could not risk them bringing the hounds to the sett, perhaps resulting in the huntsmen digging down to unearth their quarry. If necessary, Krag would drive these winter guests out by force, snapping at them with his powerful jaws. They would go. A fox was no match for a badger, teeth for teeth.

The hounds were well into the wood by now, their baying drowning even the shrieking of the jay and the chattering of the magpie. Two hares in full flight overtook the old badger. There was no time to be lost.

He was but a matter of two yards from the sett when he glimpsed Rus and Tosca. Both were already out in the open, a mixture of defiance and fear in their posture, noses to the wind, ears flat, their reddish-brown bodies poised for flight. The foxes needed no encouragement to leave the sett, and for that Krag was grateful.

Krag halted, watched. At the entrance to the sett, only his striped head showing, small eyes glinting, crouched Baal. The foxes glanced back at him, and then, with a bound, they were off through the dead bracken, their brushes streaming behind them, heading towards the northern boundary of the wood, seeking safety in the upper regions.

Krag and Baal regarded each other steadily for a few seconds. There was an expression of triumph on Baal's features, and it was obvious to Krag that the younger boar had evicted the foxes from their borrowed quarters before they had decided to resort to flight.

Krag moved forward, uncertain of himself. Baal was already staking his claim to a future leadership, and Krag wondered how long it would be before the young boar challenged him, whether the other would wait until Autumn. The friendship that had existed between them for so long was clearly over. Krag experienced sadness rather than fear. He would willingly step down to make way for his rival, but such a gesture would only serve to brand him a coward in the eyes of the colony. Nature had made no provisions for compromise, her laws were rigid and cruel. Krag's only concern was for Jetta and his wish was that the two of them might be allowed to end their days together in peace.

The hounds were closer now, their heavy bodies crashing through the undergrowth, heedless of briars and sharp thorns now that the fox scent had reached them. Baal withdrew into the sett and Krag followed him down the sloping tunnel. For the moment they were united in a common cause and only in the lower chambers would they be really safe.

Rus and Tosca were clear of the wood, running up a steep hillside. Momentarily, they were hidden from the view of the pursuing hounds, and they knew that they had to take advantage of this. Up on the skyline was another wood, much larger than the one they had just vacated, a belt of Scots pine acting as a windbreak and protecting the established oak and chestnut trees from the strong westerly winds. There was another badger sett up there, but the foxes knew from experience that they must avoid it for the occupants were much more aggressive than those they had just left. Perhaps the two foxes would lie up in the undergrowth for a while, watching to see which way the hounds went, or maybe they would skirt it and head for the fields on the other side. At the moment they did not know, for their only instinct was to flee from those who hunted them.

The leading hound, a massive brute, halted in the freshly excavated soil outside the badger sett. Nose to the ground, then head uplifted, he bayed loudly. The rest of the pack joined him, the atmosphere was heavy with scent. Two of the younger dogs attempted to enter the hole, backed off and began scratching at the ground. They whined, looked to their leader, but he was already streaking away to the north in full voice, the others behind him. Reluctantly, the young hounds followed.

Rus and Tosca rested on the edge of the big wood, panting heavily after the steep run, tongues lolling from the corners of their mouths. They looked at each other, seemed to smile in their own vulpine way. Their initial fear was gone, replaced by a mutual enjoyment of the chase. Tosca would go wherever her mate went. They could have run on now, up and over the next brow, following the course of the stream and thereby destroying their scent as they ran. They could turn off into the thick rhododendrons whenever they chose, or bask in the warm sunshine on a rocky outcrop, content in the knowledge that they had outwitted the hounds. But Rus made no move. Himself a hunter of the wild, he loved the thrill of the pursued as well as that of the pursuer. To have run now would have been too easy.

They waited.

The hounds emerged from Hopwas Wood following the uphill scent, but now their eagerness did not match their speed. They had been kennelled throughout the long, hard Winter, unable to exercise properly in the deep snowdrifts, and their stamina did not equal that of their wild quarry. Some of the younger ones slithered and slid back in places where the ground was still soft from the recent thaw. Their leader was fully twenty yards ahead of them, his heart pounding madly under the strain.

The two foxes could have taken full advantage of the cover offered before taking to the open ground again, but instead they showed themselves, trotting almost casually before setting off uphill again at a steady lope. They did not exert themselves; paused a couple of times to look back, their audacity admired by the mounted huntsmen far below, their horses lathered in sweat.

Foxes and hounds continued, humans and horses were now mere spectators to a lost cause.

Rus welcomed the ice-cold water of the flooded stream, Tosca pausing to drink gratefully at his side. From then onwards the going was easier as they followed the stony bottomed watercourse, the rushing current reviving them. Its erratic, meandering course screened them from the pursuing dogs, and at any time the hunted could have climbed the steep banks and lain in safety amidst the surrounding undergrowth. But instead they cantered on, sharing an inexplicable mutual mirth as they detected the first sounds of the pack floundering in the depths far behind them.

It was some time before Rus and Tosca left the water. They knew every rabbit track through these dense acres of rhododendrons. There was food in abundance here, even a disused earth where Tosca could rear her cubs in safety. The foxes has won from the moment they had fled Hopwas Wood. In their own way they were grateful to the Hunt, for without the pursuit they might never have returned to this land of solitude and plenty, preferring the ease and convenience of the woodlands adjacent to the farms.

Eventually, they came to a sunlit clearing where they lay down together. They could not even hear the hounds now. The pack had given up and turned back.

Rus and Tosca were safe for the coming breeding season, at least.

Chapter Three

Spring is the busiest time of the year for the badger. Every sett has to be cleaned out thoroughly, old bedding replaced by new, and every member of the colony is required to work industriously. Those entrances which have been blocked up for added winter warmth must be opened again for ventilation, and there are always new tunnels to be dug. This last task is usually carried out by the younger boars, making additional exits, for there is always the chance that Man will come with his terriers and the existing holes will be covered prior to the onslaught. Self-preservation is uppermost in all forms of wildlife, second only to the instinct for reproduction, special breeding chambers being renovated by the sows themselves in readiness for their litters.

Krag worked diligently alongside the other badgers. On these occasions there was little need for leadership for every one of them knew exactly what was required of them. Jetta, too, laboured with a will. She sensed that this could well be her last litter. Next season would be too late. Likewise, she sensed the inevitable clash between her mate and Baal, but she showed no resentment towards the young boar. It was the way of all badgers, she had witnessed the struggle for power before. It would happen again. And again. And if Krag died as a result, then she would pine and follow him. Badgers mate for life, and in the case of a female past her prime there is no possibility of taking another boar. The others would allow her to live on here in the sett, but she would have no part to play. It was all that Nature had to offer her.

The sett in Hopwas Wood went down to a depth of ten feet below the surface, its maze of tunnels covering almost a quarter of an acre. There were four galleries, the lower one used for the period of semi-hibernation during a severe winter. The one immediately above that was occupied throughout the breeding period by the sows when they were visited only by their respective boars bringing food to the mothers and young earth-pigs. During this time the males confined themselves to the second gallery, whilst the one nearest the surface was merely a thoroughfare, a defence against all but the most ardent of badger-diggers. It was in this one that the foxes were allowed to live during the winter, and during the summer it was often occupied by rabbits who seemed strangely unaware that their young were in dire peril from the lower inhabitants.

In early March Jetta gave birth to three silver-grey cubs, and Krag's time was fully occupied supplying them with food. By night he hunted, but his days were spent up on that rocky shelf above the sett, dozing but alert in case Man should threaten his mate and her young. Three of the other sows also had litters and so far nothing much had changed from previous years. But Krag's thoughts were already turned to finding a new, safer sett for the colony. Once the cubs were old enough, he would move the badgers. In the meantime, they must wait and hope that they were not molested by Man. He knew that he must take them from here before Baal made his challenge for the leadership, for the young boar did not sense the danger. Once Baal was leader it would be too late.

March merged into April, and still the accustomed serenity remained within Hopwas Wood. The gaunt trees around the sett were sprouting fresh greenery, and on the bark were new scores where the badgers sharpened their claws nightly. A carrion crow hatched her young in the old established nest in the topmost branches of a giant Corsican pine, and the cock bird hunted throughout the daylight hours to provide food for the fledglings. Like the badgers below them, these birds were paired for life, and they had used this same nest, with annual renovations, for five seasons now, successfully rearing their young each year. Perhaps Jenkins' failing eyesight had been another reason for the continued existence of the nest and its predator occupants.

Sacko, the stoat, moved down from the upper wood and began to hunt the rabbit population ruthlessly. His cousin, Pyne, the polecat, a stranger who had somehow found his way to these parts, moved into the long-vacated hole beneath the roots of a century-old oak tree, and the two animals took steps to avoid each other. Just as badgers tolerated foxes, so did polecats accept stoats and weasels. Nature does not believe in total segregation of her species.

A hen pheasant made a nest in the bracken and began to lay her eggs at the rate of one each day. For twelve days she was successful, but just after dawn on the thirteenth morning all that remained was a cluster of broken shells and a pile of feathers which wafted in the breeze. The carrion crows cawed their anger; they had spotted the nest only yesterday. Pyne was absent for a few days. He was well satisfied with his plundering.

The disillusioned cock pheasant, not the best of parents yet nevertheless disappointed, moved away to where another of his wives was having more success. He, too, was subconsciously aware of the absence of old Jenkins. Usually the gamekeeper was busy waging war on predators in the woods at this time of year. Yet, no human had set foot here since the shooting had ended in February. Further down on the farmland, when the wind was blowing from that direction, the captive pheasants could be heard calling in their pens, one cock bird with six hens in each enclosure, all part of the preservation of the species for few pheasants bred success- fully in the wild. The wild bird thought that he could do a lot worse than go down there and join them. Yet his natural instincts prevailed, and he yielded to the temptation to remain free in the woodlands.

Krag, too, had missed Jenkins. The old badger left Jetta to mind the cubs and again took to going out and lying in his favourite place of seclusion each day. The sun's rays were becoming increasingly warmer with the approach of May, and in spite of his nocturnal nature he preferred this place to the confinement of the sett. In his heart, though, he knew that he came here to keep out of Baal's way. Had it not been for Jetta he might well have wandered quietly away and so settled the issue. As it was, he knew that he had to see it through. Perhaps Baal might come to him in this solitary place one day, and then they could fight out the leadership battle away from the rest of the colony. No, Baal would want the others to witness his victory over an ageing rival.

He wondered again about the gamekeeper, but, unlike those species which needed Man's protection at this time of the year, Krag was not unduly concerned. The less he saw of human beings, the better. So, life went on, until that sunny late April afternoon when the peace which the badgers took for granted in Hopwas Wood was destroyed forever.

Krag was dozing. Above him rooks floated in the breeze, cawing raucously, and in the distance he heard the bleating of sheep. Then, that same jay which had warned of the coming of the Hunt started to screech. The magpie was chattering frenziedly. The male carrion crow glided away from the nest, leaving his mate to guard the fledglings which were almost ready to fly. The big black bird called once, and then he was gone. All around, the warning was as before.

Man. Man. Run. Hide.

Krag's eyesight being inferior to that of other creatures, he did not see the men until they were within sight of the sett. They had used the stiff breeze to their advantage so that their scent did not betray their coming, and the terriers were leashed so that they did not run on ahead and give the alarm. Fear stabbed at Krag's heart as he recognized the man at the head of the small group. *Reuben!* Warrior strained at his leash and received a vicious kick from his master. The dog whined, growled, yelped at a second kick. Three other men, each hanging on grimly to various strains of terriers, followed in the wake of the new gamekeeper. They carried an assortment of spades, nets and guns. Clearly, a full scale assault was planned on the old badger sett!

Krag moved slowly back into the undergrowth. The men had not spotted him because they were not expecting to find a badger lying out in the daytime. With surprising speed and agility he scuttled down that well worn track, his instinct that of self-survival and the protection of his mate and their cubs. Those weeks during which he had conceded the leadership to himself, awaiting the inevitable, were forgotten. No longer was he an old badger in the twilight of his life. He was Krag, the leader, again, and everything depended upon his cunning and wisdom. The other badgers would either live or die, the responsibility was his. Baal had not the experience to cope with such a crisis.

Krag went down through the first gallery and into the second where all the boars were sleeping, snoring loudly. He nudged them roughly with his snout, grunted the warning which the corvines above ground had uttered.

Man. Man. Run. Hide.

They stirred sluggishly. A set of powerful jaws snapped

angrily at him. Baal did not take kindly to being awoken so rudely during the daytime hours, but Krag ignored him and hurried on. This was no time for a confrontation. He had warned them, he could do no more. The females were his priority.

He dropped down into the breeding chamber. Some of the younger boars were following him but he did not heed them, not even troubling to glance round to see if Baal was amongst them. He made straight for the sleeping Jetta. He pushed his nose against her and she was awake instantly, surprised but not questioning. Something was wrong but there was no time to ask what, wherever Krag went she would follow with their cubs. The evacuation of the sett would not be easy, Krag knew that some of them would not make it, particularly Bru, the sow who had gone well over her time; her earth-pigs were scarcely old enough to go above ground.

Suddenly, they heard the yapping and snarling of terriers. Reuben and his badger-digging party were already at the sett, the ground below vibrating as they began hammering stout, sharpened pegs firmly into the soil. Steel scraped on stones as they started to dig. The exits were already being blocked up in order to trap the badgers below the surface.

Krag hoped that his own terror was not evident to the others. He was not afraid of dying, but the fate of the other badgers, particularly the females with their young, frightened him. Some would be slaughtered there and then, the men standing back to watch as their dogs engaged in bloody battle, others would be captured alive and taken to the city to be baited in unequal contests with ferocious dogs. Krag recalled the badger which he had found dying in the woods two winters ago, a pathetic creature whose claws and teeth had been removed, his eyes put out so that he was totally defenceless. An animal which somebody had rescued from the badger-baiters, and in their kindly ignorance had returned him to the wild where he was helpless either to defend himself or to forage for food. The badger had related tales of unspeakable cruelty at the hands of Man before it had mercifully died. Krag had not told the colony, there was no point in alarming them for it would not help them if they were captured. He determined to protect them at all costs, he could do no more. Whilst Jenkins was guardian of the woods, Reuben and his followers had been denied access to the sett. Now they were intent upon capturing the badgers which had been protected from them.

Krag hesitated momentarily. There was no escape behind, terriers and guns awaited any badger that bolted for freedom. He made his decision. Downwards, into the very deepest chamber, and he prayed that the young boars had done their Spring chores efficiently. If they had shirked them, then all was lost. Perhaps they could hold the dogs at bay for a short while, even the ferocious Warrior, but whilst they did so Reuben and his followers would be digging frantically down to reach them, cutting through any obstructing roots with axes. Ten feet of soil was no protection against men such as these.

The barking of the dogs became louder, deafening in the confined space. They had already penetrated the first gallery and were almost into the second. The excited yapping turned to yelps of pain. The dogs had met with resistance from those stubborn boars who had not heeded Krag's warning and had remained behind. Already blood had been drawn on both sides.

Krag was relieved to see that Jetta and her cubs were still behind him as he entered the fourth chamber, the largest gallery of all, with four or five different exits. Instinctively he took the one where the soil was freshest, some of it crumbling and powdering as he forced his way into the narrow tunnel. He should have checked it weeks ago, made sure that it was wide enough, that it had been completed and did not terminate in a dead end due to the laziness of some young boar who had tired of the task assigned him. In this respect Krag had failed in his own duty towards the others; all he could hope for was that his omission would not be their downfall.

On and on, fearful of what he might discover at every bend, at times compelled to use his powerful claws to scrape away an obstruction. The sounds of the battle in the upper galleries were becoming fainter and fainter. The badgers had travelled a long way and now Krag was beginning to worry because the air was becoming fouler and more stagnant. By now there should have been a draught of fresh air from the exit, wherever it was. There was none. His fears were escalating.

Another bend, this time sharply to the right. The tunnel was narrowing all the time, and once again Krag was forced to scrape away soil that had fallen in. Then he saw what he had been fearing ever since they had left the lower chamber – *a dead end*! Solid earth blocked their path, trapping them in the bowels of the sett!

Jetta bumped into him, the cubs were snuffling as though even they sensed that the escape bid had failed. Krag sank down, exhausted. They had only one choice open to them, a return to the upper galleries and certain death.

His resignation to their terrible fate lasted a few seconds, a pause in which to regain his ebbing strength. Then he began to dig, this time with an even greater frenzy. His claws tore at the soil in front of him, showering it all over himself and those behind him. He had no idea how far ahead the surface lay, or even if he was tunnelling in the right direction. Even if they made it above ground the terriers might be waiting for them. On the other hand, the badgers *might* find that they emerged into dense undergrowth with still a chance of safety. In any case, they would prefer to die above ground rather than trapped down here. Again Krag blamed himself for not checking on the work of the young boars.

His progress was slow. Fortunately, the ground was sandy otherwise it would have been a near impossible task, and, hemmed in as he was by the other badgers, his work was made doubly difficult. Jetta grunted, and with a supreme effort Krag called upon every last reserve. Had Baal been with them, then he would have conceded the leadership there and then, stood back and let the younger, fitter animal take over. Krag was forced to rest every few minutes, and during one of these pauses he strained his hearing but there was no sound from above. Either they had travelled out of earshot of the boars' last stand or else the terriers had been withdrawn to allow the men to dig down to the badgers.

Suddenly, he smelled fresh air. Even before he had broken through the final roof fall there was a warm Spring breeze blowing on his snout. His loud grunt of relief was heard and understood by those behind him. Then he glimpsed daylight, and within a few minutes he gazed up into a blue sky, dotted with fluffy white clouds, through the entwines of a thick bramble bush.

Krag forced his way into the open, moving cautiously, relying upon scent rather than his limited range of vision. As Jetta followed through the bed of thorns, the cubs in single file behind her, he realized just where the exit tunnel had surfaced. There was a small grassy hillock separating the sett from the northern fringe of the wood, and it was within a few yards of this that the lazy young boar, responsible for the greater part of that tunnelling, had ceased work. Krag had been forced to dig out about another five yards in order to bring his family and the other badgers above ground. But they were far from safety yet.

Less than thirty yards away they could hear the clink of spades on stone and shale as the men tried to reach the badgers in the second gallery. They were temporarily screened from the view of the humans, but even by moving with the greatest of stealth the badgers were sure to be spotted before they reached the open fields adjoining Hopwas Wood. Krag paused, looked to Jetta, and he knew that she would follow wherever he led. So would the others because without him they were leaderless. They must run the gauntlet of men and dogs: surprise and speed was all that was left to the badgers. They did not fear the terriers on open ground, but the men had guns and they would not hesitate to shoot.

With a grunt that was audible only to those behind him, Krag ran forward with all the speed that his tired muscles could muster, heading directly for the nearest point where the wood joined the fields.

"Hey, look! Over there! There's some of 'em got out!"

Krag did not understand the words but he knew that they had been seen. The diggers hastily threw down their spades, grabbed for their shotguns. Three deafening explosions crashed out, the reports echoing and re-echoing across the surrounding countryside. Pellets, leaden death, whistled all around the fleeing badgers. Krag felt a stinging pain in his rump, another on his broad back close to the snare. It was reminiscent of those hot, late summer days when the badgers busied themselves digging out the nests of wild bees. Nothing more. A glance behind showed him that Jetta and the cubs had suffered no worse, but at the rear of the column one of the sows was rolling on her back, legs kicking frantically in the air. Her small cubs squealed around her, they would not leave her. Krag knew that it was Bru, her immature litter had slowed her pace, kept her within range of the guns. The others had no alternative but to flee, a rescue attempt would have been futile. Sadly, there was no way in which they could save Bru and her earth-pigs.

The rest of the badgers followed blindly in the wake of Krag, they would go wherever he went because he was still their leader.

They heard more shots but by this time the animals were shielded by a dense mound of bracken, and the pellets fell short. Soon they were out of the wood and heading uphill, the incline making little difference to their speed, so accustomed were they to traversing uneven terrain.

"Get the dogs after 'em!"

The badgers were fully thirty yards up the slope, heading towards the cover offered by the adjoining woodland, before the yelping Warrior and another smaller terrier took up the scent. Warrior, for all his other faults, did not lack courage. He at once set off on a diagonal course in an attempt to head off the badgers. Odds did not matter to him. His companion followed gamely at his heels.

Krag knew that the terriers would intercept them but now it was a conflict which he anticipated eagerly. Two of the men were still watching from outside the wood, but they did not shoot again, either because the range was too great or else they were afraid of hitting the dogs.

Warrior circled, overtook the line of badgers, and stood barring their way, a low growl in his throat. The other dog joined him. Then they both rushed headlong at the oncoming badgers.

The badger leader had the advantage even though he was on lower ground. As Warrior leaped, an airborne bundle of snarling ferociousness, Krag leaned forward and met the charge with open jaws. The terrier had been bitten many times during his life of badger-hunting but never before had a set of teeth fastened on to his shoulder with such strength. In the same movement Krag flung himself backwards, releasing his hold as he rolled over. Warrior, propelled by both his own jump and Krag's throw, found himself somersaulting downhill. Yelping with pain and rage, he hurtled over the watching badgers to land in a heap, rolling in a cloud of dust, clawing for a hold but not securing one.

The second terrier was preparing to follow Warrior into the attack but now it changed its mind. Its fear rumbled in its throat as it backed off, circled, kept its distance. There was no way it was going near those badgers, especially the big one.

Two more shots rang out from the men at the bottom of the slope, but now there was no danger to the badgers from the guns. Pellets pattered on the dusty ground with no more force than that of a hailstorm. A hundred yards further on Krag turned to look back. One man was bending over Warrior, examining the dog's wounds whilst his companion was shouting in vain for the second terrier to come to heel.

Krag moved slowly on, Jetta and the cubs catching up with him. In front of them stood a huge, old established wood where the oaks and beech resembled deformed giants. It was a place Krag had always avoided in the past, not because of its forbidding appearance but because he knew it was inhabited by a colony of badgers who guarded their domain jealously, had reputedly mauled any of their own kind who had dared to trespass within it.

A barbed wire fence, some six feet in height, had been erected along its perimeter and the steel entrance gate across the rough track was heavily padlocked. A notice, red lettering on a white board, warned people to 'KEEP OUT. WAR DEPARTMENT. WHEN RED FLAG IS FLYING, FIRING IS IN PROGRESS.'

Krag had heard the gunfire in the distance many times, knew that the men who went in there used death sticks like Reuben and his friends. Sometimes they fired for hours at a time, salvo after salvo. He was puzzled, wondered what they were killing, for surely by now they would have slaughtered every living creature in this place which the villagers nicknamed 'The Soldiers' Wood'. But the men in their green and brown mottled clothing still came and shot, day after day. Certainly, this was no sanctuary for a colony of nomad badgers.

Yet they had no choice. His thoughts turned to the badgers which had remained in the sett, particularly Baal. Reuben would not give up easily. After what had happened to Warrior, the gamekeeper would take his revenge upon every badger he could find.

Warily, with the others following him, Krag pushed his way beneath the lower strand of the fence. The big wood had a sinister look about it even in the bright Spring sunshine.

Chapter Four

Two of the terriers were holding the badgers at bay in the second galley, but without Warrior to lead them neither would summon up the courage to launch a full-scale attack. Reuben was frustrated and angry when his companions rejoined him, one carrying the wounded Warrior, the other dog skulking fearfully in the background. It cringed, whined, kept its distance in case its masters tried to force it to go below ground.

"We'll dig 'em out." The gamekeeper picked up a spade, clanged it angrily on a rock. "Not one of those down there is going to get away!"

But Reuben had no intention of killing the badgers which were still holding off the other two terriers; his greed dominated his motives. There were men in the city who were prepared to pay him handsomely for every live badger he could deliver to them, men whose cruelty exceeded even his own. The 'sport' of badger-baiting was illegal but very lucrative. These people risked imprisonment and heavy fines, but they paid good money. A smile crossed the gamekeeper's face; he tried to estimate how many badgers might still be below ground. This could be a very, very profitable venture.

The snarling, barking terriers backed out of the nearest hole. They flopped to the ground, one pawing at a bleeding ear, the other licking a gashed leg. Warrior whined his sympathy from the arms of the man who held him and the fourth dog slunk even further away. None of them had any intention of going back down below to face the cornered badgers again, not even if their masters thrashed them. Reuben had never before known Warrior defeated, and it was quite obvious that the others would be of no more use today.

Baal huddled in the third gallery with the other badgers who, along with himself, had spurned Krag's warning. All of them bore visible evidence of the recent battle, for their attackers had inflicted several nasty bites in spite of their inferior size. Now the young boars were looking to Baal for guidance, but he avoided their gaze and stared down at the sandy floor. He tried to hide his fear. For months now he had dreamed of defeating the ageing Krag in combat and taking over as leader of the Hopwas Wood colony. The result of that encounter he had presumed to be a forgone conclusion. Now he was not so sure. Krag was old and slow moving but today he had demonstrated stamina and wisdom which the young animal found disconcerting.

Until now Baal had not given much thought to the responsibilities which he would be taking on as leader. It did not end with the supervision of renovating the sett each Spring, the gathering of winter bedding, and the constant foraging for food to ensure that none went hungry during the long spells of severe weather. There was much, much more to it than that. The safety of the colony was paramount, their leader had to be cunning and brave if they were to survive attacks such as had taken place today. Krag had done just that, escaped with his followers. Baal was not sure how the other had achieved this, he had regarded the retreat to the lower galleries as a show of cowardice. Now he wished that he had led these young boars in the wake of his rival.

He thought about it for some minutes. Perhaps there was still time to escape, a chance to retrieve any faith that had been lost in him.

Without so much as a grunt he began the descent into the lower regions of the sett. His every movement was uncertain, indecisive, and the other badgers did not fail to notice this. They watched him go, but they made no move to follow him. If they had heeded Krag, they might have escaped. It was preferable to remain where they were rather than to let Baal lead them into further danger. They had no confidence in his leadership any more. It was he who had persuaded them to stay, whilst with Krag they might have made it to freedom. They crouched there in the darkness, fearing the return of the terriers. They might be able to drive them off again, but in the end their enemy, Man, would triumph. They listened to Baal's progress until at last they could no longer hear his shuffling movements. Now they had none to look to for guidance, and when the next attack came it would be every badger for himself, powerful jaws against snapping, relentless teeth, and eventually their stubborn resistance would be worn down.

Baal reached the deepest chamber and lay down, breathing heavily. He realized that his bid for leadership had been rejected by the badgers up above, that he had lost any respect which they might once have had for him. Likewise, the same applied to those who had escaped with Krag, they would not support him against one who had led them to safety. *If* they had made it to freedom. Baal was utterly alone, and now the strongest instinct of the creatures of the wild predominated – self-survival.

He regarded the various exits. His powers of scent told him which one Krag and the others had taken. He moved towards it but changed his mind at the last moment. The furthermost one, dug by himself two seasons ago, came out in a silver birch thicket some distance from the sett. He knew its every turn, and he was reluctant to try an unknown passage. This way he would be screened from men and dogs, then once above ground he must rely on speed, run the gauntlet of terriers and the sticks which made loud bangs and meted out pain and death. He moved slowly, afraid to go on, but even more frightened to stay behind.

The passage began to rise steeply upwards. A current of air ruffled his coarse hair and he sensed freedom around the next bend. Then daylight dazzled him, made him blink, and he had to wait whilst his eyesight adjusted to the brightness. He wished that night had cast darkness over the land, it would have been so much easier. And safer. The Spring sunlight frightened him almost as much as the men and dogs who waited for the badgers to show themselves. Baal listened, heard movements, heavy booted feet and voices, but they were some distance away, over by the main entrance to the sett. A terrier whimpered, and the sound restored some of his waning courage. That dog, at least, had no stomach for a fight.

He crawled to within a yard of the exit, and with the sunlight still blinding him, Baal envied Krag those long hours above ground which had doubtless accustomed their leader to daylight. Krag had used his wisdom where it mattered most. Even so, Baal knew every inch of this woodland by scent alone, and he was aware that by travelling due north he would eventually come to the big wood from which there was nearly always gunfire. He feared to go there, but he had no choice; he would use it merely as somewhere to lie up, a place in which to regain his strength and courage before travelling on. Somewhere, some day, he would find the place he was seeking, a disused fox earth, or a rabbit warren which he could enlarge to his own liking. There he would remain in solitude, an outcast, until perhaps he came upon others of his own kind who had not heard of Baal the coward, the deserter. Then, possibly, he might challenge for leadership again.

Thus Baal reflected upon the future which lay ahead of him, but, above all, he realized that first he must escape from here. He closed his eyes, called upon every aching muscle in his young body, and then rushed blindly out into the open.

The fresh breeze met him, thorns tore at his coat, bracken flattened beneath his weight. Then, suddenly, he was rolling over, caught and held by some unseen adversary, his legs and head entangled so that he could scarcely move them. His first thought was that he had blundered into the thick patch of briars beneath which the rabbits had their warren, relying upon the barrier of sharp thorn for protection from predators, but what held him was smooth and strong, pinioning every limb, and pulling tighter with his frantic struggles. He opened his eyes, saw the familiar landscape around him through a maze of squares. He bit at them, but they were too smooth and fine for his sharp teeth to secure a hold, slipping from his jaws, sliding between his claws so that he was unable to scratch and tear at whatever it was that enveloped his entire body. He lost his balance and rolled over on to his broad back, kicking feebly like a cast ewe. Man-shouts came to his frightened ears, followed by vibrations of running feet, and the barking of terriers that hung back behind their masters because their memories were still fresh from the recent encounter.

"There's one in the net!"

Reuben was first on the scene, closely followed by the man who still cradled the wounded Warrior in his arms. The terrier struggled, snarled, and it was all that the man could do to hold him.

"It's a beauty. Fetch a sack. There's fifty quid in that net!"

Baal ceased to struggle, not simply because the large purse-net had by now rendered him totally helpless, but because he had already resigned himself to his fate. These men would kill him; he just hoped that the end would be quick, preferably from one of the sticks which made loud bangs and dealt out instant death. He closed his eyes, waited. But nothing happened, there was neither a noise nor brief pain. After a few seconds he squinted at the scene around him in the dazzling Spring sunlight.

Warrior was still being restrained with difficulty, whilst a third man had appeared on the scene who was now unrolling a large hessian sack. Reuben was handing him a length of bright blue string. Baal did not understand what all this was about but something told him that they were not going to kill him. At least, not imminently. His fate was beyond his understanding, and all the more terrifying for that.

The sack was laid on the ground, one end lifted up and held open. For a moment Baal scented human fear; his captors were afraid of him.

"Hold that sack wide. Get ready to close it as soon as 'e's inside."

"Watch 'e don't bite you.'

"'E won't get the chance. Now, let me catch 'old of the brute!"

Reuben reached inside the net, gripped Baal by the rear legs, strained to lift the badger, manoeuvering the animal up out of the nylon mesh until his head and shoulders dangled inside the neck of the sack. Then all was dark for Baal, he gasped for air in the cloying, suffocating atmosphere. With unexpected suddenness that hold on him was relinquished, catapulting him into the depths of the bag. The opening was closed and tied, imprisoning him even more securely than the net had done. Impenetrable blackness engulfed him, he struggled briefly, then lay still again. He could scarcely breathe; his claws snagged the clinging folds but did not rip through them.

Seconds later he felt himself being dragged along the uneven ground, stones scraping sharply on his body. The bumping jarred him, winded him and made it even more difficult to breathe. He did not understand what was happening to him, only that his captors were taking him away somewhere. For what purpose? Every few minutes they paused to rest, taking it in turns to pull the cumbersome sack. Baal heard them talking, laughing. Far rather would he have remained in the besieged sett and died in his own surroundings.

The men's progress was becoming slower. It was a long way back to the gamekeeper's cottage and Reuben had made a wide detour, avoiding public rights of way, keeping to the hedgerows, in case they should be spotted by some inquisitive villager. But they saw nobody, and it was late evening before they finally arrived at their destination.

Baal's keen sense of smell picked up a stale, musty atmosphere that filtered through the sack, and his bruised body felt the unaccustomed smoothness of an artificial surface beneath him as he was finally deposited in some closed place. There was a scraping noise, followed by a dull thud, and then he could hear human voices no more. He had no idea where he was, he had ceased to care. He presumed that he had been dumped in some place of human habitation and left there to die a slow, suffocating death. After a time he dozed, his usual alertness deserting him.

Some time later he was awakened from his exhausted, fitful slumber. He sensed a human presence. The man was alone, and he knew it was Reuben for there was no scent of fear. The gamekeeper's companions had been afraid of the badger.

Once more Baal was on the move. The sack was pulled roughly out into the open air and the badger knew from the cold dampness of the atmosphere that night had fallen. Again he longed for the freedom of the woods, the scuttling of frightened mice amongst the carpet of fallen leaves, and . . . He forgot everything as he became airborne, landed with a thud on another flat surface. This one was different, it had not the coldness of a stone floor. His nose twitched at familiar and unfamiliar odours. Terriers, ferrets, other smells which were alien to him. Something slammed metallically, and he sensed from the echo that he was enclosed in an even smaller space than previously. He scented Reuben only a few feet away, and then came the most terrifying, clattering roar that rose to a crescendo. The floor beneath him shuddered and vibrated, began to move, a jolting and swaying that had him rolling inside the hessian prison. His sensitive lungs were filled with choking, pungent fumes. This was surely the end, death by suffocation, in the same way that once a smaller colony of badgers in the wood had been gassed by Man!

His prison outside the sack was moving, smoothly at times, roughly at others, and throughout the journey that roaring and clanking continued. Baal was confused, they could have killed him up there in the wood but instead they had chosen to submit him to this inexplicable terror. He was familiar with the distant sound of cars and tractors around his habitat, and on one occasion he had only just been quick enough to scramble up a steep bank in time to avoid oncoming headlights and wheels that would have crushed the life from his body. But he did not associate those strange moving objects with his present confinement.

Suddenly, everything was still. They had stopped, the roaring noise whined to a silence. There was another clang, and he sensed that Reuben was no longer close. Even stranger still, Baal was alive and unharmed. But he was more frightened than ever.

Time passed. At length he heard voices and approaching footsteps. Fresh night air penetrated the roughly woven hessian, dispersing those obnoxious fumes. Baal remained motionless, fearing what might happen. Reuben was talking to another man, and although Baal did not understand what they were saying, he knew only too well that they were discussing him.

"You won't get one better'n this 'un," Reuben said. "Took some catchin', I can tell you. They'll pay well for a boar like this."

"Let's 'ave a look at 'im." The other voice was older, hesitant.

The sack was dragged roughly from the rear of the van, the bump as it hit the ground winding Baal again. It was Reuben who grasped the neck, dragged it a short distance until Baal felt another cold, flat floor beneath him. There was light, too, one that came from neither sun nor moon, shafting inside as the string was untied. Gloved hands seized the badger, pulled him out by his hind legs, held up upside down. The men were wary of snapping jaws, but Baal was too dazed to offer any resistance.

"Slip that muzzle over 'is 'ead," Reuben grunted, and before Baal realized what was happening a set of leather straps had been slid on to his muzzle and tightened. A clinking jangle was his only warning of the chain collar and leash which followed it.

Reuben was breathing heavily from the exertion as he lowered the badger to the floor and wound the end of the leash around a supporting post in the centre of the spacious implements shed. "'E's a fair weight, they don't come better than that one, I can tell you!"

Baal crouched down on the floor, afraid of these two men and dazzled by the artificial light. He made no attempt to move. All the fight had long gone from him.

"Hmm," Davies, the farmer, regarded their captive with a stoic expression. He no longer relished the prospect of passing on Reuben's catches to the man from the city. Once it had meant a few easy pounds. Now the rewards were more lucrative but the penalties were severe if you were caught. His own cut, he decided, did not warrant the risk. He had hoped that the gamekeeper would not bring him any more badgers.

"Well?"

"I dunno. Nobody's asked me for badgers lately. They might not want them any more."

"'Course, they will!" Reuben was shocked, angry.

"'Ow much are you goin' to give me?"

"Thirty pounds."

"Thirty! They're fetchin' up to a hundred these days."

"You go and get your hundred, then!"

Reuben fell sullen, stared at Baal. He did not want to keep the animal around his own cottage; the shooting syndicate members called from time to time and if they saw a captive badger the gamekeeper would be sacked instantly. Likewise, he did not know of an instant market, he had always relied upon the farmer to sell his catches for him. "It's 'ardly worth the trouble."

"Thirty quid, or you can take 'im back, let 'im go."

"All right," the gamekeeper's tone was subdued. Thirty pounds was better than nothing. "*This* time. But when you've sold 'im, I can get some more. I'll be in touch in a week or so."

The men left the shed and the light was switched off. Baal had not understood, but he sensed that his fate had been determined. They were planning something for him and he was very frightened.

He lay down, rolled over and pulled at the muzzle with his sharp claws. This caused the collar around his neck to tighten, had him choking and gasping for breath. He stretched himself out on the concrete floor, lay with his pointed snout resting on his feet. That one single attempt to free himself had destroyed his will to escape. In his own way he resigned himself to whatever fate lay in store for him. He would never return to his native woodlands, his way of life had been snatched from him the moment he had blundered into that net. Never again would he listen to the wind sough-ing through the branches, ruffling his fur as he hunted rod-ents and dug for roots, the moon rising over the pine tops and bathing the landscape in its silvery glow. All that he had taken for granted was gone. Forever. But no matter what these men did to him, they could not destroy the call of the wild. He would pine, and eventually he would die.

After some time Baal slipped into an uneasy slumber, his ears habitually tuned to the faint sounds around him. The sparrows and starlings jostled for roosting places in the eaves, mice and rats scurried amongst straw bales. Occasionally a pair of tiny eyes focused on him, perhaps pitying him in his plight, but none approached him. Chained as he was, he was still their enemy, a badger which preyed on their cousins in the wild. These creatures had a different reason for being in Farmer Davies's outbuilding. Above all, they could come and go as they pleased. This was their environment, they had learned to live alongside Man, adapted to his ways.

And they still had their freedom.

Part Two

SUMMER

Chapter Five

Whilst Baal was being transported in a hessian sack to his new life in captivity, Krag led his badgers into the Soldiers' Wood. Sometimes, during his nocturnal rambles across that tract of open ground that bordered this sinister wood, and which served as a rifle range for the troops from the barracks just outside the city, he had chanced to meet badgers from this place. A grunted warning and nothing more passed between them, and then each hurried on their separate ways.

Krag accepted that no friendship was asked or given, that he would have been spurned, possibly attacked, had he attempted to strike up a relationship. Even Rus kept to his own territory and did not trespass upon that of another fox. But where Man is concerned, there is a natural alliance between all species of wildlife. The jay and the magpie screeched and chattered their warnings of approaching danger for all to heed, friend and foe alike. Thus it was that Krag sought help in a time of trouble from these remote badgers. Not necessarily a permanent home but a brief resting place, a disued fox earth or a rabbit bury in which they could seek refuge before moving on elsewhere. Before the frosts came again he hoped to find that place of which he had only distant, infant memories, his own birthplace from where he had wandered to join the Hopwas Wood colony many seasons ago. His recollection of it was so faint that it might only have been a figment of his daytime dreams and, in reality, it had never existed. He recalled an acreage of hardwood trees standing starkly on a steep hillside amidst a sea of dense undergrowth, truly a wooded island, over which his own father had ruled.

He had not, so far, spoken to Jetta about his intention of finding it again. It could well be that, if there was such a sett, then over the years it had been filled in by a succession of Spring thaws when the muddy soil had run down into the tunnels and blocked them. Or, worse, a fierce badger colony occupied it and would repel any trespassers with fang and claw. Or, perhaps, foxes lived there. Or else there was no such sett, never had been. Krag would not know until he had searched for it. Some strange instinct told him that it lay up in the hills beyond the Soldiers' Wood.

As they made their way through the tall pines it was soon evident to Krag that a large number of badgers inhabited the Soldiers' Wood, far more than he had at first thought. The undergrowth was thick but the tracks were many. A maze of runs traversed the dense briars, and there was no doubt that in this strange wood the badgers were the supreme rulers. Flattened bracken, brown crushed fronds from the previous year and snapped green shoots of new growth, denoted the area where the cubs played. Many of the tracks led from this clearing into the deep woods, disappearing beneath a huge rhododendron thicket, an invincible barrier against human trespassers, a sanctuary for those who sought only peace and solitude.

Although the sun had still not sunk behind the western skyline, there was little difference between day and night in here, for its rays penetrated only the clearings. In Winter, gigantic flocks of starlings migrated here from Russia, took up residence in the rhododendron forest. The foliage was weighed down with their droppings, the foul stench permeated the entire wood, many of the shrubs becoming poisoned by this pollution, and dying. Then, with the advent of Spring, the intruders returned to their native land and the rains cleansed their deserted habitat. It was a cycle which would go on for many years.

Once, Man had attempted to move them in Midwinter, fearing lest their foulings might contaminate an underground reservoir close by. The soldiers who used the adjacent firing range for target practice sent up flares and rockets in an attempt to divert the starlings from their impenetrable roost; farmers provided shotgun battues until their gun barrels were too hot to hold. All to no avail. Waves of chattering birds darkened the late afternoon sky, wheeling round, defying every attempt to repel them, finally breaching the human defences and dropping down into the heart of the rhododendrons where they twittered their mockery of mankind long into the night hours.

After that the flocks were left in peace, repugnant as their migratory roost was to farmers and the water company, whose fears were discovered to be unfounded when the water supply was proved to be clear and pure. So, like the badgers which inhabited the Soldiers' Wood, the starlings, too, were left unmolested.

Krag moved steadily on, following the widest track of all as it twisted and turned back on itself a score of times before emerging into yet another large clearing amidst the trees. The wandering badgers gazed in awe, for here was a badger sett of unbelievable magnitude, freshly excavated mounds of soil denoting an architecture that was in itself a subterranean animal city, the planning of which had been undertaken in the days when Krag's great-grandfather was but an earth-pig. They had staked their claim then, and they were still here now.

Krag came to a standstill, the others huddling around him. Even the cubs were silent. The old badger sensed that this was not the sett he sought, his own birthplace, for the location was not as he recalled it from his misty memories. This was a mighty colony of old established badgers who would not greet strangers kindly. He experienced a humility, and had he and his followers not been exhausted from their recent ordeal and flight, he would have skirted this place.

He waited. To have entered any of those tunnels would have been an act of sacrilege. They would do so only if they were invited by the inhabitants, and that in itself was unlikely. They would be asked to explain their intrusion and, if this was accepted by the occupants, then they would have to abide by the laws of their hosts. Most likely the nomads would be told to continue on their way, to travel far from here, but Krag was not prepared to subject Jetta and the cubs to further rigours without some attempt to find a temporary resting place while they regained their strength. They would sleep out above ground, if necessary. Then they would continue their search for his own birthplace. More than likely they would not find it.

Deep dusk merged into darkness, and still they waited, every one of them uneasy because they feared the badgers who lived in this dark and gloomy Soldiers' Wood; where the atmosphere was heavy with a stench of decaying vegetation, where not even an owl dared to break the deep silence; where every bird and beast lived in awe of their rulers.

The moon had risen above the pinetops before Krag saw a movement in one of the entrances to the sett, a striped head bathed in sinister shadow regarding the newcomers in an ominous silence. Doubtless their arrival would have been heard, for badgers are aware of any movement above their habitation, either by day or night.

The watching badger made no move to emerge into the open. Krag became increasingly uneasy. There were probably others watching them, too, a myriad of unseen, hostile eyes looking out from the darkness of the sett. He moved closer to Jetta; he would protect her with his life if they were attacked. The cubs sensed danger, huddled up against their mother. The rest of the badgers also closed in, instinctively seeking safety in numbers. Perhaps they were already doubting their leader's wisdom in bringing them to this place.

More heads became visible, but none came forward to greet the strangers. It was as if they were waiting for something, perhaps their own leader to return after a dusktime search for food to appease his gnawing hunger.

Finally, a badger appeared at the top of the steep, sandy bank above the sett, shambled down to where a single shaft of moonlight filtered into the clearing. It was a powerful creature, larger than the average-sized boar, but it was not so much its size as its sheer malevolence that had Krag pressing back against his mate. The creature just stood there, looking at those who had dared to trespass in its domain, its small eyes glinting with suspicion and hostility.

Krag felt Jetta begin to tremble, and her fear aroused his protective instinct, boosted his waning courage. She was silently asking him to safeguard their cubs, sensing the danger as much as he did. Without her, he might well have withdrawn as gracefully as his pride would allow, apologized for their intrusion. Instead, he stood his ground, meeting the gaze of this malevolent badger. There seemed to be badgers watching them from every direction now, surrounding them in case they attempted to escape. And from somewhere in these deep, dark woods came the mournful 'oooh-oooh' of an owl. It, too, feared for the safety of the wandering badgers. Not so much as a dead leaf rustled in the night breeze, as if this fearsome creature was gifted with a power as mighty as that of Nature herself.

The big badger moved closer, his powerful body rippling gracefully with every muscular movement, his small, deep-set eyes never once shifting from Krag. He advanced another shuffle, jaws agape and seeming to grin evilly, displaying the wicked tusks with which he had won his own battle for leadership in some long past encounter. He stopped. Only inches separated the two animals, and Krag braced himself in readiness for an attack, stood his ground even though he realized that he would be no match for this brute in combat.

Suddenly, the whole clearing came to life, badgers moving out of their tunnels into the open, ringing the strangers as if they had been trained to surround any who infiltrated their kingdom. There were others on the slope, more of them along the fringe of rhododendron bushes. Watching and waiting.

Krag estimated that his party were outnumbered by at least three to one, and any false move could result in instant, merciless death for himself and those with him. He regretted his decision to come to the Soldiers' Wood, but it was too late now. Somehow, in spite of his misgivings, he affected an air of surprise and mild indignation at this reception, for a show of fear might be as disastrous as one of aggression. His only course was to state his case, relate the recent happenings, and rely upon the age-old code of the creatures of the wild in their alliance against Man.

It was not easy for there was much to tell, and communications between animals, even of the same species, is reduced to a series of basic noises and signs, for their need to converse, unlike humans, is seldom necessary. Never before had Krag faced a more difficult and dangerous task, the massive badger watching him fixedly throughout his narrative. It was plain that these badgers in the Soldiers' Wood had even less knowledge of Man than their Hopwas Wood counterparts. Sometimes, on their foragings, they glimpsed a farmer, and they took steps to avoid contact. Never had they experienced an attack on their sett. Their habitat was not included in the acreage rented for shooting by the city syndicate, and although these animals heard the distant gunfire, they had no cause to seek refuge whilst beaters and dogs drove the pheasants from the undergrowth to the waiting sportsmen. This colony had progressed little during their lifetime, and they had inherited their mistrust of all outside badgers from their forefathers in this closely-knit sett.

Krag's speech was a lengthy one, and by the time he had finished the silver orb in the sky above was already waning. He told them about Reuben, an evil man, a sworn enemy of all badgers, one who might find his way *here* one day. The audience of badgers shifted restlessly in unison, a sign of mirth and ridicule. *Nobody*, Man nor beast, would dare to interfere with them! Not wishing to contradict and anger them, Krag continued with his story, describing how he and his family had escaped, along with his loyal followers, and how several of them carried shot in their bodies. One of their party had been killed by the guns, he emphasised. The listening circle moved in closer, looking for wounds to confirm this story, suspecting a lie until they noted the flecks of dried blood on the newcomers' coats. They would not have tolerated lies, a story invented by a bunch of homeless badgers with the intention of joining an old-established colony would have resulted in instant death.

Krag concluded by asking, without humiliation, for temporary shelter for his party, time in which to search for a more permanent home elsewhere. He made no mention of his birthplace, for if there was such a secluded sett, and these animals knew of its whereabouts, they might claim it for their own expanding colony. Then he sank back on his haunches, satisfied that he had done his best, and that there was nothing more he could do to determine their fate.

At last the large badger broke his own silence. He began by telling Krag that *no* badgers from outside were welcome in the Soldiers' Wood. It was an ancient law, and during his own lifetime he could recall no instance when it had been broken. But there *were* exceptions, left to the discretion of the leader, and he, Dul, ruled over *all* living creatures in these woodlands. Even Rus would not trespass here, except perhaps to pause for a brief rest in the undergrowth when the Hunt was pursuing him. Nevertheless, Man was their mutual foe, even though he seldom troubled them, and it was possibly the snare around Krag's body which swayed the issue in the latter's favour. Also, Dul delighted in an audience, and here were some badgers who had not before heard accounts of his own feats of bravery, an existing ruler and an ambitious challenger both having perished at his jaws in regal combat. Then there was Kino, the Collie, whom Dul had fought and killed. Innumerable other exploits poured forth from Dul, the ruler and boaster, and throughout them Krag waited anxiously for the other's verdict. But it was not forthcoming until the eastern sky was turning pale and the sinking moon had lost its brilliance.

Yes, Krag and his badgers could remain in the Soldiers' Wood, but only until the leaves began to brown . . . but there were a number of rules and conditions which they must agree to observe during this time. Dul resented another leader residing within his own kingdom, however small the sett over which that animal had held sway. Therefore, an oath of allegiance by Krag was demanded. Likewise, his followers must regard themselves as being subservient to the resident badgers. Their place was to serve, and before they finally departed, it would be their duty to prepare the entire sett, with its many galleries, for the coming winter. When that task was completed, they would be allowed, compelled, to leave. A return, at *any* time in the future, carried a penalty of death!

In the meantime, chambers would be provided for them, and the boars would be free to forage in search of food at night. The Soldiers' Wood was a place of plenty in that respect. Dul, in his wisdom, knew that the boars would not attempt to escape under cover of darkness and leave their females to pay the price for their desertion.

It was full daylight by now, and Krag was exhausted. Jetta leaned her weary body against his, not caring that her mate had given his oath to serve another ruler. If any of the others understood, it mattered not to them, for this was the price of survival, and they realized that without Krag they would now either be dead or in captivity, victims of the badger-diggers' cruelty. The Summer would soon pass, and then they would leave, their cubs fully grown, and their period of enslavement would be nothing more than a distant memory, another chapter in the history of a badger colony which Man had driven to seek refuge elsewhere.

By sunrise the Hopwas badgers were sleeping soundly in their borrowed quarters. Whilst in the valley below, Baal was beginning his first day in captivity. In the space of a single day, a way of life that had gone on peacefully, decade after decade, had been changed.

Chapter Six

*T*he weeks passed. The days became longer and hotter and the skies remained cloudless. The sheep in the fields bordering Hopwas and the Soldiers' Wood survived on a diet of straw-like grass, and even the rushing stream, which had its source in a rock fissure up above the woods, was reduced to a steady trickle.

Krag feared for the safety of his badgers; he would only know peace of mind when they were away from this place and free of their overseers. The work delegated to them by Dul and his council was finished, and now the days were spent sleeping and the nights hunting for food.

Jetta did not appear to be unduly concerned. The cubs were weaned now and able to fend for themselves. By night they caught voles and young rabbits and dozed with her during the daylight hours. Krag was dreaming of that place where he had been born; sometimes he could see it more clearly than others, the small wood high up on the hillside, a kind of dry land island surrounded by bracken and scrub. He thought he sensed its nearness, recognized some of the tracks which he had used when he was a cub. But probably it was no more than wishful thinking. He wondered if he would ever find it again. Already he was wishing the Summer away, eagerly anticipating the shorter days when the first sugary frosts glinted on the pine trees. He was aware, though, that Dul was watching him closely. Too closely.

Dul did not trust Krag. Although this was not surprising in such a large, remote colony where strangers were seldom, if ever, allowed to visit, the other's constant vigilance worried Krag. He wondered about the reason. Fear? No, Krag was in no position to undermine the leader's authority. Jealousy? No, Krag had his own mate with him and, especially now that the breeding season was over, he was unlikely to turn his attention to any of the other sows.

Nevertheless, he detected a smouldering hatred in the ever watchful eyes of the ruler of the Soldiers' Wood. Wherever he went, he sensed that he was being followed, a faint rustling of the undergrowth as he hunted for voles, shrews, mice and young hedgepigs. It might have been his quarry stealthily eluding him, but he knew that it was not. Dul would lie for hours in the entrance to the large gallery at the top of the sandy bank, just watching Krag's comings and goings, those malevolent, tiny eyes never leaving the old badger.

One warm, moonlit night, Krag wandered further afield than was his custom. The young rabbits and voles were becoming scarcer than he had known since his arrival in his new surroundings. He blamed the dry weather, the creatures seeking moisture down on the farmlands where there was piped water for sheep and cattle. The growing cubs were demanding more and more food each day, so he explained to Jetta that it would be necessary for him to increase the range of his nightly excursions. The moon was full, and he decided that with an early start, soon after dusk had fallen, he could return to his old haunts and be back in the sett before dawn broke.

Jetta did not approve of her mate returning to Hopwas Wood. She feared Reuben, and there was the added risk of the gamekeeper's snares and traps set in the hedgerows around the farms. But Krag was insistent, explaining that it was the only way in which he was going to be able to meet the demands of the hungry cubs. They could hunt for themselves, but they were too young to traverse any distance. Reluctantly, Jetta agreed, begging him to be careful. He assured her that his wariness had not deserted him even though he was past his prime, but he chose not to confide in her his worries over Dul. Dul was much, much more dangerous than Reuben.

Krag left the sett at deep dusk, and as he headed downhill away from the Soldiers' Wood, he knew that he was being followed. The moon had not yet risen, and he neither saw nor heard the faintest of movements behind him, but that instinct so vital to survival in the wild told him that Dul was on his trail. It could have been one of the other boars with instructions to follow him and report back on his movements, but he knew in his heart that it was the leader himself, that it was Dul who skulked on his spoor, seething with an inexplicable hatred, a mounting fury raging in that powerful body. Krag had given up trying to find a reason for it, he just hoped that the Hopwas badgers would be away from this dreadful place before the wrath of Dul exploded into bestial savagery.

Krag skirted Hopwas Wood. He was tempted to enter and hunt the familiar landscape for old times' sake, but again his instincts warned him not to do so. His reluctance to re-visit his former territory was not due entirely to a fear of Reuben or the traps and snares which the gamekeeper would surely have set. It was simply that he could not bear the thought of gazing upon the devastation, the desecration of his former home, evidence of the slaughter which would doubtless have taken place after his escape and, above all, the fact that Man had at last conquered the woodlands.

A feeling of sadness crept over him as he lay in a patch of

gorse just outside the wood. It had always been a good place in which to surprise an unwary rabbit. After dark the coneys emerged from their burrows to graze the fields, searching amidst the scorched grass for a patch of lush green that had been shaded from the direct rays of the sun and which they had overlooked on the previous night. But tonight there was not a sign of a rabbit. Perhaps the weather conditions had forced them to change their feeding habits, and they were now grazing later, towards dawn, when a slight dew would provide them with enough moisture to survive yet another day of cruel, blistering heat.

Then Krag heard a movement in the gorse behind him. It stopped. He listened intently for some time before he heard it again. Whatever it was, it was too big for a rabbit. A rabbit would have squeezed silently beneath the spiky foliage; it would have neither the need nor the physique to force a path through the densest parts. The same applied to the bloodthirsty stoats and weasels, so it had to be a creature of considerable size. Krag's nose twitched. There was no scent of fox. His unease mounted.

Then, some distance above him on the parched slope where the gorse bed ended, he picked out the striped, pointed head of one of his own species, its body hidden from his view in a patch of shadow. Every muscle in his body tensed, and he experienced a brief moment of sheer terror until he saw with relief that it was not Dul. The head was not broad enough, the eyes were too far apart. Suddenly, the other saw him, and as it shuffled in his direction Krag recognized the approaching badger. It was Shaf, one of the young boars who had elected to remain in the sett that day with Baal in a last desperate stand against Man and dogs.

Shaf seemed pleased to see Krag, and any enmity which the younger creature had borne him during the early Spring, when he had sided with Baal, was now gone. Both were eager to hear news of how their respective parties had fared, and for a time hunting was forgotten.

Krag told him all about the Soldiers' Wood and Dul, and Shaf became decidedly uneasy, glancing back uphill from time to time, a furtiveness about him which alarmed Krag. Perhaps Shaf had heard of Dul, but if so, he did not mention the fact. The younger badger went on to relate the final episode of the seige of the Hopwas Wood sett, told how Reuben had called off his terriers and was seemingly satisfied because they had captured Baal alive. And, Shaf added, Baal was surpisingly still very much alive and well.

Shaf had been to visit Baal down at Davies's farm only two nights ago. The badger was still chained up, of course, and lived in an old dog kennel in a corner of the farmyard. He showed no animosity towards either the farmer or his family, and meekly accepted food from the children's hands. There was contempt in Shaf's eyes when he reached this part of the story. Baal, the savage young boar, whose ambition once had been to overthrow Krag, was now reduced to the status of a pet dog. He did not even have to hunt for his own food!

A few of the badgers still lived in the old sett. Reuben had not returned since that day for he had been far too busy rearing pheasants in the paddock behind his cottage in readiness for the coming shooting season. The badgers stayed on, although they posted a sentry, day and night, in case the men should return.

A sow who had lost her mate in a cruel, illegal steel trap, had joined them. She had given birth to three earth-pigs and the others felt obliged to remain with her until her young were big enough to move elsewhere. Then they would all leave. When Autumn arrived, there would be no badgers left in Hopwas Wood. It seemed to Krag that they were all waiting for the Autumn when there were going to be many changes, many comings and goings.

Soon afterwards Krag and Shaf parted company, each returning to the business of hunting. Wildlife certainly seemed more plentiful down on the lower slopes, and just as the first faint streaks of dawn were appearing in the eastern sky, Krag was back in the Soldiers' Wood, carrying four young rabbits which he had dug out of a shallow warren in a thick hedgerow. It was certainly no feast for a growing family, but at least the cubs would survive until the next night.

There was no sign of Dul although most of the badgers were preparing to retire below ground to shelter from the long hot day which was just beginning. Just as Krag was about to go down to join Jetta, the huge leader lumbered into the clearing. Their eyes met, and Dul issued a low, warning growl. Krag remained silent, for to have answered would have been to accept a challenge. Instead, he turned his back and made his way down to the chamber below. The fearsome ruler had threatened him, for no apparent reason other than that animals sometimes take an instant dislike to each other. It could have been the heat. All the same, Krag sensed that Dul had followed him throughout his long trek back to Hopwas Wood.

Krag handed over his catch to Jetta and their offspring. He had eaten when he had killed, it was easier than carrying his own meal back to the sett. He made no mention of either Dul or Shaf to his mate.

Yet, Krag had felt safer away from here; when Dul made his move it would come within this very clearing, for the badger leader would not wish the encounter to take place without an audience. One moment Krag would be dozing, the next he would be fighting for his life; and that of Jetta, their cubs and the badgers who had come here with them.

Krag slept for much of the day, and when the cool of evening aroused him from his slumbers, he knew that if he was again to provide food for his family then he must return to those fields bordering Hopwas Wood. Another idea occurred to him, he would visit Baal at Davies's farm. It would not be far out of his wanderings, and he bore his former rival no animosity. He would like Baal to know that, too. Both of them had suffered humiliation following the raid on the sett, and it might be of some comfort to Baal if he went and talked to him.

Chapter Seven

Krag left the sett even earlier than he had done on the previous evening, and without glancing up at the topmost hole on the bank, he knew that Dul was watching him. Would the big badger follow him again? Krag increased his speed until he was well clear of the Soldiers' Wood.

The moon, being later each night, would not be rising for another couple of hours yet, and he welcomed the deep shadows that hid him as he took the shortest and steepest route towards Hopwas Wood. He would go and call on Baal first and hunt for rabbits on the return trip. Tonight there was no sign of Shaf, nor any of the other badgers, but his instincts told him that somewhere in these wooded hills Dul watched and waited. But how much longer was the leader prepared to wait before he threw down his challenge?

Krag had never been into the very heart of human habitation before. Always, in the old days, he had skirted the farm buildings, dogs barking as they caught his scent on the night wind, and only when he was well away from the outbuildings did he feel secure. When he had first decided to go and visit Baal, this fear had not even crossed his mind. Now, as he paused on the fringe of the sprawling, dilapidated barns and outbuildings which surrounded the small, white-washed farmhouse, the old feelings came back, even stronger than previously. Yet, this time there was something different, an eeriness which puzzled him until he realized what it was. There was total silence; even the dogs did not bark, and the place seemed devoid of life.

He had almost decided to turn back, to go and hunt rabbits in the fields, when his ears caught the faint clinking and rattling of a chain in the shadowy farmyard. The gentle breeze which blew towards him brought with it a scent which he recognized immediately, the smell of badger, the odour of his own kind. Of course, that was the reason why the dogs had not barked. They had become used to the presence of Baal, and to them one badger was much the same as another. The chain tinkled again.

Baal was restless tonight. The moon was now a deep, orange ball above the distant pines, and it doubtless brought back sad memories to the captive badger, a yearning to forage and hunt again in the surrounding countryside. Nature was calling, but Baal was unable to answer her summons.

Krag moved stealthily into the untidy yard, instinctively taking advantage of any available cover, creeping from shadow to shadow, afraid to venture too close to the tractor and other rusting farm implements, their symmetrical outlines representing a harsh artificiality that was in frightening contrast to the silhouettes of trees and hedges.

Baal's kennel had housed three generations of sheepdogs before he had been confined in it. The woodwork was rotten in places, the narrow entrance had been chewed by playful pups, but the vertical deep scores on the outer walls had not been made by any dog. Even in captivity, Baal still had the habit of sharpening his claws; he did not have access to tree trunks any longer, so he made use of his own dwelling. Most likely, though, Krag reflected sadly, those claws would never again dig out a nest of young rabbits or scratch for beetles in the ferny floor of the woods.

Baal grunted in surprise when he saw Krag, stared for several seconds in disbelief. Shaf visited him from time to time but he had never expected to see the old badger leader again. His surprise was quickly replaced by something else, a lowering of his head, glancing anywhere but at his visitor in a sudden show of embarrassment, a rarity in the wild, something which animals always interpreted as weakness. Krag did not; he pitied the other, but to have shown this outwardly would have been regarded as an insult. Fang and claw was the badger code, no quarter asked nor given. That was the way it would have been had their clash for supremacy come about.

The tethered badger was grateful for the opportunity to talk with another of his own kind. Certainly, he enjoyed Shaf's infrequent calls, but nothing new was happening in Hopwas Wood these days, and Baal had wondered how Krag, and those who had escaped with him, had fared. He shook his head slowly from side to side when he heard about their temporary summer home in the Soldiers' Wood. Dul . . . Dul? The name was vaguely familiar. He had heard it mentioned somewhere but he could not remember where. Perhaps it would come back to him later. In the meantime, though, he related the details of his own capture, and how he came to be at Davies's farm. Of course, he did not understand *why* Reuben had brought him here, but he much preferred the farmer to the gamekeeper.

Soon after Baal's captivity had begun at the farm, some men had arrived after dark one night. Davies had brought them to look at the badger. An argument had resulted, voices raised and fists shaken before they departed in their vehicle. The badger did not understand what it was all about, but he sensed that the disagreement revolved around himself. Those men had not returned, and from then on Baal was kept chained in the yard, out of sight of the house and any who chanced to call.

The farmer was rough but kindly, and his children were always bringing food out to their new pet. Too much, in fact, and Baal was afraid that he would become fat and lazy, and if ever the day came again when he had to hunt for his own good and fend for himself, he feared that he might not be able to readjust to the natural way of life which he had once known.

Krag studied the chain by which the other was held. It was fixed to a ring in the wall. The ring was rusty and the brickwork was crumbling with age. Eagerly, he pointed this out to Baal, certain that if the two of them pulled together, exerted their combined strength, the chain would be ripped free. It might even snap under the strain. But Baal shook his head slowly. He had no wish to escape!

Krag was amazed. It was beyond his understanding. However, Baal went on to talk about humans and their ways. He had not mastered their language yet, but he had been with them long enough for him to be able to denote from their tone of voice, and from the way they frequently gestured with their hands, what they were talking about. They weren't all like Reuben, he told Krag. Which reminded him, Reuben had been here only yesterday. Baal had retreated into his kennel and grunted a warning when the gamekeeper had come into the yard to look at him. Then Davies had appeared on the scene, and the two of them had talked for a long time. Reuben had constantly pointed up towards the hills, way above Hopwas Wood, and Baal sensed that the conversation was about badgers. Finally, the men had gone into one of the buildings. Reuben had come out carrying a couple of massive knives with curved blades, and a small axe, much smaller than those used by the woodmen that week following the mighty gales when some fallen trees had to be cleared from the lanes.

Baal was puzzled; the talk was of badgers, yet what use were knives and an axe too small to fell a tree? Krag did not reply, but he was uneasy. The time was right for Man to capture badger cubs that were weaned and could survive without their mothers yet lacking cunning so that they were easily captured. *And where better to find such earth-pigs than in the Soldiers' Wood?* The only obstruction was that dense wall of rhododendrons which surrounded and protected the sett from intruders, where the starlings roosted in winter and fouled the land with their droppings. And Reuben was a very determined man, greed spurring him on to anything which he had in mind. Large knives and a small axe would cut a path to the badger colony . . . with ease!

Baal talked on but Krag was not listening. He was thinking of Jetta, their cubs, and the other badgers which he had led to safety from Hopwas Wood. Now their freedom, their lives, were threatened yet again. They had not seen the last of Reuben, evidently. And Dul, what would *he* do about it? Krag knew that he would have to warn him immediately upon his return. Unless, of course, Dul was at this moment lying within earshot, listening. But even if he was, he would not understand, for he had lived a remote life and was not wise in the ways of humans. Krag must tell him, before the sun rose, so that plans could be made for evacuating the sett. Reuben and his friends might come any day now. Even tomorrow.

Krag left, telling Baal that he would return soon. First, there was food to be found and then the badgers must be warned of the danger. The latter was a task that Krag did not relish.

The dogs began to bark as Krag left the farm. They had picked up an unfamiliar scent; it might have been Rus checking on the henhouse during the course of his nightly prowl, hoping that a stubborn bird had decided to sleep out in the open rather than in the confinement of a stuffy building on a warm night. Krag hurried on, he had more important matters to attend to.

As he reached the lower slopes, a movement along the opposite hedgerow attracted his attention. He stopped, his own markings a perfect camouflage against the straggling hawthorns. He strained his eyes, and then he saw something emerge from the shadows into a patch of moonlight, a small reddish-brown creature, similar in many respects to Sacko, the stoat, yet half as big again with a long bushy tail. The creature covered the ground in swift, jerky bounds, then stopped as its keen eyesight picked out the old badger.

Krag was only too familiar with Pyne, the polecat, the voracious little hunter who had his home beneath the deep roots of that gnarled oak tree in Hopwas Wood. Pyne was a stranger in a strange land, having travelled here in stages from the Welsh foothills seventy miles from here, the homeland of his species until his wanderings brought him to these woodlands. There was food in plenty here, an abundance of rabbits, and he had no reason to move on. Krag did not know the reason for the other's presence here, he had never enquired simply because he was not interested. They knew each other by sight but had never paused to converse. Pyne had no fear of Reuben, and unless he foolishly stepped into one of the latter's cunningly concealed traps, then life would go on as before for the polecat. A loner, seldom seen by Man, he, too, was a nocturnal hunter, and he enjoyed the freedom of the countryside unmolested.

The polecat was carrying something in his mouth, a dead barnyard rooster almost as large as himself. He was half-dragging, half-carrying it, taking it back to his lair to feed at his leisure, leaving a trail of feathers in his wake. He continued on his way, satisfied that the skulking figure watching him was only a harmless badger.

Down below at the farm the dogs continued to bark. Krag wondered if it was because of Pyne, or whether Rus was still prowling restlessly, unaware that his intended prey had already been snatched from beneath his jaws. Krag kept to the shadows, but there was no further sign of Pyne. The polecat was using every scrap of available cover on his return trip, and only the sudden erratic flight and angry calling of a disturbed nesting peewit denoted the route which the polecat had taken. After a time the bird returned to its concealed nest in the middle of a field. Tonight it was safe; tomorrow it might be in danger for Pyne had a long memory, and he would know how to save himself that trip down to the farm to fetch another rooster.

Krag located a nest of young rabbits, fed swiftly, and then set off uphill with the remainder of his prey clutched firmly in his jaws. It was full daylight by the time he returned to the clearing in the Soldiers' Wood. The majority of the badgers had already retired below ground. There was no sign of Dul, and Krag wondered whether the other was already sleeping or if he was still trying to locate the trail which he had lost at Davies's farm.

Krag's first duty was to deliver the food to Jetta and the cubs. She moved aside for him to lie beside her, but for once he declined her invitation, and made his way back up to the clearing above. He did not relish his meeting with Dul, but the safety of the sett depended upon him convincing the leader of the danger which threatened them all.

He lay down, blinked in the early morning sunlight. He was exhausted after his foray but he dared not sleep.

Chapter Eight

The clearing was empty, there was not a badger in sight, no sign of life on the sandy slope beneath which Dul and his council lived. In all probability they were already sleeping and to awaken them would invite their wrath upon any who dared to disturb them. But there was only one course open to Krag, their very existence depended upon it.

He climbed the bank wearily, his feet slipping because the drought had made it difficult to secure a foothold on the steepest places, until he came to that yawning entrance which led into the bowels of the mighty sett. He shrugged off his fear, for had he not been a ruler, also? Indeed, he was still the leader to whom his own badgers looked in times of danger. In his prime he had been as strong and as powerful as this Dul, as eager to take on any challenger. He had had many memorable victories, too. If anything, he had been a better leader than Dul, for he had shown compassion towards those over whom he had governed. With these thoughts to boost his courage, he entered the huge assembly chamber far below the rhododendron roots.

The badgers were holding council. Dul was seated on a mound of hard packed earth, a rostrum from which he looked down upon the dozen or so who sat and regarded him with undisguised awe. Pheasant feathers littered the sandy floor along with skeletons which had been picked clean of every vestige of flesh. Krag's sweeping gaze took in all this, and he knew only too well where these badgers had hunted during the nocturnal hours. Whilst he had been diligently searching for rabbits and voles, Dul and his followers had carried out a daring raid on the game preserves, ruthlessly plundering the rearing fields where Reuben housed his semi-tame pheasant poults. Doubtless, they had left a trail of wanton slaughter behind them, and Reuben would be in no doubt concerning the identity of the culprits. Much as he hated the gamekeeper, Krag realized that this night of carnage would only serve to bring the wrath of the cruel man upon them all. Krag could not condone the actions of these badgers; only toothless, senile animals, no longer able to hunt or dig for edible roots, resorted to poaching. It was the code of the wild, and these renegade badgers had broken it.

It was some seconds before they became aware of Krag's presence, so intent were they upon listening to Dul's boasting of their night of slaughter. Then, they realized that there was an intruder in their midst and they turned as one, jaws wide, eyes smouldering with fury, and only a sudden grunted command from Dul prevented them from launching themselves upon Krag. They stopped, and Krag, who had crouched instinctively to meet the attack, was made even more aware of the power which this mighty boar wielded over his subjects.

Dul remained on his raised platform, his eyes seeming to glow redly in the darkness, surveying the scene before him. His next command would be one of life or death to this stranger who had dared to enter the sacred council chamber. But Dul was in no hurry, he savoured such a situation, all the time building upon the legend which he had created for himself.

It was Krag who spoke first. If necessary he was prepared to die, to be ripped apart by these vengeful creatures, but it was his duty to warn them even if it went unheeded. In his own way he told them of the raid planned by the gamekeeper, the way in which the supposedly impenetrable barrier of rhododendrons surrounding the sett would be breached, and that in all probability it would happen today, before the sun set. He declined to add that they had brought Reuben's fury upon themselves by their greedy and foolish act.

The badgers shifted uneasily, looked at Dul. Such was their awe of their leader that they believed him to be invincible, a match for any, Man or beast, who dared to enter their kingdom. Dul ignored them, turned his gaze to Krag and there was scorn in his expression. When he spoke, it was to his followers, ignoring the one who had disturbed their meeting.

He reminded them of his compassion towards the nomad badgers, his generosity in allowing a leader of another colony into their midst even though the condition imposed was that this one must obey and serve a far mightier ruler. Instead, Dul added, his eyes glinting, this Krag had been plotting against them secretly. In fact, the coming of the homeless badgers was all part of a devious scheme to overthrow this colony. Of course, he, Dul, had seen through it, and he had merely been awaiting the opportunity to quell the rebellion. The badgers from afar feared those in the Soldiers' Wood, knew that one day Dul and his council would rule over the entire surrounding land, and so they had conspired to overthrow them. They had sent forth a small band to infil-trate the big sett and erode its power structure from within. First, they knew they must usurp Dul, the most formidable task of all, and this very creature who now crouched in their midst had his own designs upon the leadership.

Now, Dul added, the Hopwas badgers sought to trick the colony into a hasty evacuation of the sett with lies of an intended raid by the gamekeeper. Had not he, Dul, proved to them last night that his cunning was more than a match for Man, leading them on a raid on the game preserves The gamekeeper would be more concerned with repairing his damaged pens and taking steps to prevent another such raid than coming *here*. Had they had the misfortune to have a leader less wise than himself, then they might well have been tricked into abandoning the sett, and when eventually they sought to return, intruders from afar would have taken over the sett and been in a position to prevent them regaining their home. As a result, the age-old strain, the *original* badger, would die out and be replaced by mongrel rabble.

Krag did not reply, there was nothing more that he could have said. He had told them the truth, and in return this evil one had used the warning to further his own sense of power and cunning. The badgers grunted their admiration for Dul, they were ready to obey any order which he might issue. They scented blood!

However, Dul was not finished yet. Always eager to take on another in regal combat, he saw an opportunity to establish his position even more strongly, and so put off that day when a strong young boar might decide to challenge him for the leadership. He saw in Krag a comfortable victory, a demonstration once again of his own might at the expense of one who was not *visibly* past his prime.

A grunted order sent two of his subjects on their way to summon the rest of the sleeping colony. He would not wait for nightfall, they would fight *now*, in the clearing above, in full daylight, and the plot to take control of the sett would have failed miserably.

Then, when the moon rose, the rest of these infiltrators, and their cubs, would be put to death!

Chapter Nine

Krag was partially dazzled by the bright sunshine as he faced his enemy. The badgers had clustered into a circle around the two contestants; those from the Soldiers' Wood trembled with excitement, their Hopwas counterparts with fear. There could be only one outcome. Even Jetta accepted this as she attempted to screen her cubs from the spectacle with her body. It seemed only yesterday that she had resigned herself to such an outcome with Baal. It was the law of their kind but this was so unnecessary. Krag had done his best to warn this savage colony of the danger they faced and his reward was to be brutal death, for it was inevitable that he would be the loser. Nevertheless, she prayed that her mate would give a good account of himself, leave a few scars for Dul to remember him by.

She wondered what would happen if by some miracle Krag managed to defeat his opponent. These badgers would not let him take the leadership, they would cut him down, outnumber him and rip him to pieces. And afterwards they would probably fight amongst themselves to decide who should rule the colony. No way would they tolerate outsiders. Jetta found herself hoping that Reuben might come and exact revenge on her behalf. No, she would not wish that on anybody, not even these blood-lusting badgers. Anyway, she had her cubs to think about.

The air was filled with excited grunts from the watchers as the two badgers circled each other warily. Even Dul was not foolish enough to risk a headlong rush, for Krag's jaws were still powerful and his claws were needle sharp. They feigned blows and bites, attempted to lure their opponent into action. Dul was confident, arrogant; Krag was resigned to his fate but determined to leave his mark on the other before the end came.

Jetta saw that already there was pain and weariness in Krag's body. The wire noose beneath the fur seemed to have tightened, restricting his breathing, whilst the old gunshot wounds smarted intolerably. His long trek down to Davies's farm added to his tiredness. But whilst all this slowed his reactions, it also dulled his body somewhat to further pain, so that the first slashing blow which raked his side did not push him into instant retreat. Instead, Krag struck back with almost equal force, catching Dul by surprise and off balance, rolling him over in a cloud of dust. Krag seized on his advantage, and then the two of them were locked together, tusks seeking a throat wound, claws raking the coarse coats. The first blood was drawn.

Over and over they rolled, combat skills transcended by ferocity and resilience. From now on sheer strength alone would be the deciding factor.

Once Krag felt his teeth closing over Dul's throat, but before he could close his jaws the other somehow twisted his head to one side, and all that the old badger achieved was the satisfaction of ripping a mouthful of hair from his opponent's skin. Dul retaliated with a ferocious shoulder bite, but Krag dislodged the hold with a slashing claw.

The sun climbed high over the tall pines but still they fought. Krag was tiring fast now, and Dul was only too aware of this. It was just a matter of time before he wore this intruder down. Even so, he had not anticipated such difficulty, and unless he ended it soon his mythical invincibility would be in doubt and this might result in other council boars challenging for the leadership. At the very least it would undermine his rigid rule over them. His position and his pride were at stake.

Suddenly, Dul secured a hold which Krag was unable to break. The big boar's teeth clamped on his neck, too high for a lethal bite but forcing his head slowly back. Unless he yielded, Krag knew that his neck would break. Somehow he straightened his body, both animals standing on their hind legs like battling grizzly bears. And then it was all over. Krag was catapulted on to his back, lying with his feet kicking feebly in the air, eyes closed and awaiting the inevitable.

Dul dropped back on to four legs, shambled forward and stood over his beaten foe, tongue lolling out of his open mouth, his coat matted with blood. Excited grunts came from the watching badgers. Jetta turned her head away, attempted to distract the attention of her cubs. They would learn as they grew up; one day their turn would come, too. On the other side of the clearing Dul's followers were grunting impatiently for him to end it. They would not be satisfied with less than death.

Dul waited whilst he regained his breath, and then, to the amazement of his subjects, he turned and began to address them. Again he sensed an opportunity to turn a situation to his advantage. Badgers, like other animals of the wild, despise weakness, but together with strength they admire the quality of mercy. As Dul knew only too well.

He spoke again of the plot against them which *he* had foiled, and reminded them of the necessity of killing the Hopwas badgers when the moon rose. Yet, this Krag, Dul emphasized, was old and weak and far better that he was executed along with his fellow plotters than remembered as a martyr killed in a battle for the leadership.

Dul stood over his defeated opponent and began to make light of his victory. It had been all too easy, if he had wished he could have defeated him at the outset, but how often did these badgers have the opportunity to witness a bout in which their leader participated? It would be many seasons before he was ready to defend his position. For to kill Krag now would be akin to devouring a nest of newly-born rabbits. Let him die ignominiously with his fellow-schemers!

His speech was greeted with noises of approval, for who dared to question the undoubted wisdom of Dul? After he had lingered beneath the applause, Dul ordered that the captive badgers be confined to their quarters until the moon was directly over the Soldiers' Wood. Then he shuffled back up the sandy bank, desperately trying to hide his agony from those who watched him go. Only he knew how badly he was hurt, and he hoped that a long sleep in the coolness of the deep sett would revive him before darkness fell.

Jetta lay beside Krag, her rough tongue licking at his wounds, straining to turn him over on to his feet. His eyes met hers and it was all that she could do to hide her relief from the others. He was hurt, but not seriously. They had but a few hours left, anyway, and her only consolation was that she would die alongside her mate. If by some means she could have got the cubs to freedom then she would not have cared.

Badgers pushed at them with their long snouts, snorting angrily. Dul had commanded that these traitors be confined below ground until the hour of their execution, and that meant *immediately*, wounded or otherwise. Unceremoniously, they herded Krag and Jetta down to the prison chamber.

Krag flopped down in the cool darkness, Jetta still caressing his wounds, aided by the cubs who did not understand.

73

With his eyes he thanked her in his own way, and she believed him when he told her that he had hurt Dul much more than was apparent. Strangely, Krag felt more at ease than he had done for the past few weeks. He had done his best for the Hopwas badgers, he could not have done more.

Dul had sentenced them to die, and his guards were stationed at the only exit to ensure that the prisoners did not attempt a mass escape. There was no time in which to dig another tunnel, and, anyway, their captors would surely have heard them. Krag's only regret was that he had not instructed some of the young boars to work secretly on one soon after their arrival here. It was too late now, they must accept their fate.

The sun rose higher, its heat scorching the already parched hillsides. Lower down, sheep moved into any patch of shade which they could find. A sparrow hawk rested on a fence post for it was too hot to hunt today. Woodpigeons clustered in the pines, preferring a shady daytime roost to foraging for food in the fields. Some turned their attention to the bilberries which grew in abundance on the shaded, woodland rides; the fruit was not yet ripe but it offered moisture and filled their crops.

The grey squirrels spent most of their time nowadays in Davies's overgrown and neglected orchard where the small fruit seldom reached maturity, devouring the leaves as well as the scrubby apples and pears.

A magpie sat in the shade of a silver birch thicket on the fringe of the Soldiers' Wood. Even in the intense heat, he would raise the alarm if danger threatened. Several times he had announced in his own inimitable way the presence of Pyne, Sacko and Rus. Life in the woods was unpredictable. Safety one day, sudden death the next.

Some time during the late afternoon the magpie spotted a party of men climbing up the slope from Hopwas Wood. He noted the terriers, and recognized the guns as instruments of death, for he had miraculously survived three seasons of plundering the game preserves. He continued to watch their progress for some time, then he gave his harsh, chattering alarm call, and flew off over the brow of the hill.

Chapter Ten

*K*rag stirred restlessly in his sleep. The bite from Dul's jaw throbbed incessantly, but his senses, especially his hearing, were as keen as ever. Vibrations carry a long way below ground, especially when the surface has been baked hard by a long heatwave. His ears picked up the sound of booted feet, scurrying dogs, and he knew without any doubt that the badger-diggers were here.

He roused himself, poked Jetta with his snout. He was surprised that he could still move with a reasonable amount of agility, the stiffness was the worst but hopefully it would wear off. Instructing the others to remain where they were, he slowly made his way out of the chamber and up the tunnel until he could see a circle of brilliant daylight ahead of him. He waited patiently for his eyesight to adjust to the brightness, and then he was able to make out the shapes of the badger sentries dozing in the shade of the overhanging rhododendron bushes. None of them stirred, perhaps he was mistaken and he had dreamed it all. He remained in the entrance to the tunnel, watching for a while, for there was nothing any of them could do whilst the guards were there.

Then he heard the barking of excited terriers some distance

away, and the steady slashing of axes and machetes on obstructing undergrowth. Krag did not wait to witness the reactions of the badgers in the clearing but returned immediately to Jetta and the others.

The Hopwas badgers were huddled in the chamber, looking to Krag for guidance for now they, too, had heard the men and the terriers. In a way the arrival of Reuben and his friends was a relief, a diversion, for the animals had already resigned themselves to death. At least they might now have a chance.

In a single file the badgers followed Krag back up that tunnel. He stopped a yard or two from the entrance, blocking the view of those behind him.

It seemed that every badger had come up into the clearing, bunching together in the centre. They were clearly terrified, looking around in bewilderment, not understanding the sound of human voices, yapping dogs or the hacking blades which were slicing their way through those rhododendrons which had provided the creatures with a sanctuary for so long. Once again, Krag reflected, they were going to be forced to move on in search of quieter places. If they escaped.

The sentries which had been ordered to guard the imprisoned badgers had deserted their posts, joined the milling throng of their colleagues. Jetta pushed at Krag but he still held back. Even in a time of crisis he doubted the wisdom of joining forces with their enemies. There was always the possibility that Dul might order their execution there and then, revenge taking priority over safety in his mood of crazed rage. But there was not a sign of Dul. He had not yet emerged from his regal chamber, and without his leadership his subjects were in a state of blind panic.

Krag poked his head out of the hole and squinted up at the opposite bank. At the very moment he saw Dul; the huge badger had crawled out of the sett, was squatting on the ledge, watching those below him, clearly puzzled. But this time there was something different about him; it showed not only in his awkward posture but in those eyes which usually glowed with fury. Now they had a glazed look about them, as if Dul was at a loss to understand the situation, let alone take command.

The leader struggled further out into the open and a brief sensation of triumph flooded over Krag as he saw the other's coat, bare in places, the rest matted with dried blood. Dul had been far more seriously wounded than ever Krag had dared to hope.

Dul attempted to stand but flopped back down again. The watching badgers huddled still closer, for now it was clear, even to them, that the one who had ruled over them for so long was mortally injured. They looked for a command but it did not come. The members of the council glanced uneasily at one another. They desperately needed a leader right now but this was no time to contest one.

Without warning a snarling, barking bundle of fury burst through the bushes. Warrior had arrived, and on his heels were the three other terriers who had fought the badgers in the Hopwas Wood sett.

Warrior halted, hackles erect, teeth bared, a low growl in his throat. Even he would not face such odds, but he knew that his master and the other men were not far behind. Their guns would throw this badger army into disarray, then the terriers would rush in, darting to and fro, snapping, biting, dodging the deadly teeth before choosing their moment to move in for the kill.

Somehow Dul managed to haul himself up, but the effort was too much for him and he slumped back to the ground. He lay on his stomach panting for breath, avoiding the dis-mayed looks of his subjects. Already he had conceded the leadership, he hoped that death would be swift, that he would not have to suffer further humiliation.

The men were almost into the clearing, hacking frenziedly

at the remaining branches which impeded their progress. Reuben was yelling to the terriers to "hold 'em there!"

Suddenly, the badgers fled, an ungainly retreat towards the opposite side of the clearing, away from the advancing men. The terriers darted in pursuit, barking and snapping but keeping their distance for a badger had the ability to turn swiftly.

Never before had Warrior come upon so many badgers above ground, particularly during the daylight hours. Almost always the skirmishes took place down below, cornering, harassing, holding their foe at bay until their masters dug down to them. This was bewildering, a situation which confused and excited the terriers, causing them temporarily to forget their training.

The clearing was deserted. The surrounding rhododendrons were filled with the sounds of crashing, fleeing bodies, grunts, barks and general disarray. One of the younger terriers yelped with pain as, in his eagerness and inexperience, he closed in on one of the council boars. He had forgotten the lesson he should have learned on the previous encounter in the lower wood.

Krag moved swiftly, broke into a run, Jetta and the cubs staying close to him, the latter not understanding what was happening but sensing that they must follow their parents. Only once did Krag glance back, one final look at the now pathetic figure of Dul, alone up on that rocky outcrop. Their eyes met briefly, and Dul showed his teeth in a snarl, but it was merely a final token of the hatred which was ebbing from him. Krag understood the other's feelings, and in a strange way he pitied him that sense of defeat. Far better would it have been for the big badger to have remained underground in his chamber. At least that way his followers would not have known that his victory over his adversary was but a brief one. Then he could have died with dignity.

There was no time to be lost, and in spite of his stiff and

aching limbs, Krag picked up speed. He took a path to the right of the one taken by the fleeing badgers. Already the noise of battle was receding, and in all the confusion nobody was likely to worry about his own small band of nomadic badgers. Nevertheless, he was relieved to gain the cover of the bushes where he came upon a well-used track leading downhill.

Reuben forced his way through the last of the rhododendrons, his craggy features shiny with sweat. He was muttering angrily to himself, cursing Vinny, the broad-shouldered man immediately behind him who had been responsible for unleashing the dogs before they reached the sett.

"Never know'd badgers to lie out on top o' the sett in daylight before," Vinny gulped his excuses for, in spite of his size, he was afraid of the gamekeeper.

"Well, you've mucked it up proper this time!" Reuben snarled.

"Maybe there'll still be some below ground," Vinny's tone was subdued, the nearest he ever came to apologising for a mistake. then, "Hey, look up there!"

Reuben followed the line of Vinny's pointing finger. On the summit of the bank above them lay the largest badger the gamekeeper had ever seen. It was at once apparent that the creature was badly hurt although its snarling jaws denoted that it would not give up without a fight.

As they stood watching, the other two men joined them. One already had his gun raised but Reuben seized the barrels, and pushed them skywards.

'No!" He hissed. "Let the dogs 'ave a go at 'im!"

"And where are the dogs, then?"

There was little doubt concerning the whereabouts of Warrior and his companions. The four men stood and listened to the crazed barking, the frequent yelps of pain, and the heavy crashings which came from the bushes all around. A running battle was taking place, and they knew that the fleeing badgers had the advantage; size and strength in open combat, and a lifelong knowledge of the maze of tracks through the dense undergrowth.

The men settled down to wait, knowing that the terriers would return only when they chose to do so, when every badger had out-fought and out-witted them. And throughout, the badger up on the slope stared down at an enemy which he had not encountered before. Man. Dul knew that his end was near, that whatever they chose to do to him, it would be too late. He had not the strength to crawl back into the sett, but he would not concede defeat without a fight if they came for him. His teeth were as strong and as sharp as ever, and his bite still remained.

Time passed. The sounds of battle had long since died away. The youngest of the terriers was the first to return, slinking back into the clearing, an ear torn and dripping blood. It cringed, fearing another beating from Reuben. Then it saw the badger, whimpered and cowered. It had no desire to fight again today.

The other dogs came back at intervals, every one of them bearing evidence of their defeat. Warrior was last, limping on three legs. The injured limb had a deep gash down its whole length. But Warrior never gave up. He had given as good as he had received, and the badgers had only escaped because there were too many of them. His head went up, he scented Dul, saw him and gave a low growl. Immediately the terrier's injuries were forgotten and he was struggling uphill towards his hated enemy.

"Go get 'im!"

Reuben's shout sent the other three terriers in the wake of Warrior. They kept well behind him, though, for they were afraid of the wounded badger and they knew that their scarred and bleeding champion would do most of the fighting. Indeed, he resented their presence at the kill. Injured as he was, he would battle to the death.

Warrior was too experienced to make the mistake of attacking Dul from the front. He challenged his foe, dodged the fearsome lunge of those jaws. He circled warily and then, without warning, he leaped on the badger's back. Dul, unable to turn his head, grunted his pain as sharp teeth sank into his neck, but his cunning had not deserted him. Somehow he summoned up the strength to roll over, taking full advantage of the steep incline, and in that same moment Warrior was forced to relinquish his hold as the crushing weight threatened to break every bone in his body. Dul rolled, slid down the bank with the other dogs snapping at his rear as he went. Finally, a clump of gorse checked his fall and he lay panting, still defiant.

Warrior struggled to his feet, shook himself, his agony forgotten in his fury. He pushed his way through the other three who were biting at the badger's rear quarters, barked at them to stand back. Warrior had a score to settle with Dul. No badger had ever rolled on him before.

Reuben watched apprehensively, regretted his rashness in ordering his already battered terrier in for the kill. Once he was tempted to drive Warrior off with a stick and order Vinny to shoot the badger. But his cruelty prevailed; he wanted to see a fight to the end. He was confident that the dog would be the victor.

Warrior never made the same mistake twice. This time he did not jump on Dul's unprotected back even though they were now on level ground. From hereon it was fang versus fang, canine speed matching badger strength, and all the time the latter was weakening.

Dul snapped viciously but his teeth closed on empty air, every lunge was weaker than the previous one. Finally, Warrior darted in, seized the broad throat and sunk his teeth in deep, shook the striped head from side to side until there was no retaliation left in his adversary.

Dul was glad that he had gone down fighting, but even as

his life ebbed from him, he knew that it was not the vicious terrier that had defeated him. Krag, the Hopwas badger, had triumphed in the end, and by right the old boar was now ruler of this sett. Yet, that would never be, for already the end of this ancient badger stronghold was nigh.

Reuben and his comrades picked up their spades and started to dig, choosing those places where the ground was soft and sandy, avoiding the shale structures. In spite of his exhaustion and his wounds, Warrior was desperate to go below ground, anticipating abandoned cubs in the lower chambers. Eventually, Reuben was forced to tether him to a nearby tree. If there were cubs down there, then he wanted them alive and unharmed. This time they would not be sold to Davies, for the gamekeeper had met some men from the city who would pay his asking price for badgers against which to pit their fighting dogs.

The sun reached its zenith and there was a silence in the Soldiers' Wood except for the clinking of spades on stones and shale. But the diggers' labours were in vain for Krag and the Hopwas badgers were already far from this place.

Part Three:

AUTUMN

Chapter Eleven

Krag and those with him heard the sounds of battle in the rhododendrons behind them and hurried on, anxious to be away from the Soldiers' Wood as quickly as possible. They followed well-worn badger tracks and after some time they arrived at a belt of tall, windswept pines. The heat and the dazzling sunshine tempted them to lie up in the thick bracken and rest beneath the cool fronds until night fell, but there was still danger in these woodlands for them so they struggled on.

Once away from the wood the ground rose sharply, its dusty dryness as slippery as ice. Sure-footed as the badgers were, they slid back frequently and their progress was slowed. But there was no pursuit, no sign of life at all. Even the magpie sentinel had deserted his territory, for the Soldiers' Wood was no place in which to linger.

Krag was a leader once more and there was none to challenge his authority. Fate had granted him an extended period of rule for it was necessary for the survival of those who looked to him for guidance. He would not be challenged again until the following year now, and in the meantime there was much work to be done.

He wondered where the other badger colony had gone,

how many of them had escaped death or capture. In all probability they would split up and roam the woods, each family claiming its own small territory now that Dul was no more. Krag's thoughts turned to the birthplace which he remembered so vaguely. His instincts told him that it lay to the north of here, way beyond the Soldiers' Wood. How far, he did not know, but he knew that if he saw it he would recognize it for it would be as he remembered, a sett that was older even than the one from which they had escaped.

They came upon a stream just as the sun was setting and paused to drink from the cold, clear water. This spring would never dry up, no matter how long the drought persisted, for its level had barely fallen. Then they climbed again until they came to a scrubland plateau, an expanse of level ground high above the wood from which they had fled. Over to the west, shimmering in the rays of the dying sun, lay the city with its three-spired cathedral, a human habitation so cut-off from this remote landscape that it might as well have been a thousand miles away.

Krag decided that it would be best for them to spend the night hours amidst the undergrowth here, to regain their strength and stay until the following evening. They chose a thick patch of gorse, for its wicked spines offered protection against any who might follow them up here. Beneath its foliage they found a fox-earth but they ignored it for it smelled of recent use. Little did they realize that Tosca, the vixen, had reared her cubs here, and only a few days ago the family had gone their own separate ways. Rus had returned to the fields whilst Tosca had headed north. Only when the snows came would her nocturnal screams lure him back, and then their cycle would begin again. So would the fully grown cubs find mates, too.

A night and a day passed. The rabbits here were unwary, having remained unpersecuted for so long, and the young boars caught enough to feed them all. The earth-pigs, too, were learning fast, and it would only be a few weeks before they were able to fend for themselves.

Krag was grateful for the respite. He slept for much of the time, and again Jetta soothed his wounds with her rough tongue. Strangely, it was the old snare beneath his fur which troubled him most as if it was tightening still further. His breathing was laboured and he was very tired.

However, with the coming of dusk on the second night, he felt refreshed enough to continue. Even though the heat was still relentless by day, he scented a change in the atmosphere, a dampness that brought a welcome dew after nightfall. Autumn was already stealing over the parched countryside, almost unnoticeably, ready to take over from the long, hot summer.

Krag led the badgers even further into the wooded hills. None asked where they were going for they had absolute faith in him. Only Jetta guessed.

Night after night they wandered on, hunting, searching, the young badgers growing stronger all the time. The moon grew until it was full again, an orange ball rising above the small spinney that was known as the Devil's Dressing Room, turning the hills silvery as it climbed high in the sky. Once the night was filled with the clamour of a skein of Canada geese as they passed over on their way to feed on the stubble fields beyond.

It was on one such moonlit night that Krag paused at the foot of a gently sloping hillside. He had nearly given up hope of finding his birthplace and was searching for some deserted fox or rabbit earth in which they could shelter from the cold of winter, when he saw the small wood, its tall oak and beech trees silhouetted against the skyline, the details obscured by shadow. New life seemed to course through his weary body and he knew, without any doubt, that he had found that which he had been seeking.

He broke into a shambling run; the others, even Jetta,

watched in surprise. This wood was silent, not even an owl announced the arrival of the badgers. Their feet rustled through a thick carpet of leaves, the residue of many Autumns, dried out by the long hours of sunshine during the Summer. A dead world, steeped in mystery, trees that had survived the gales of a century of Winters, their deep roots refusing to relinquish their hold. For this was the place the distant villagers referred to as 'The Hanging Wood', not because it hung upon a hillside but because Cromwell was reputed to have hanged a hundred Royalists here; a gloomy place that some whispered was haunted, and where ghostly corpses swung from creaking branches on windy nights. But the badgers knew nothing of the legends of Man.

Krag recognized it as surely as if he had been here only yesterday, the mounds of earth between the boles of the mighty trees, the entrances to the sett partially filled in by soil that had washed down from the banks, curtained by dewy cobwebs, proof that neither fox nor rabbit had moved in. This was a place in which his own species might well have originated. He wondered why his father had left and taken the colony on the long journey down to Hopwas Wood.

There was much work to be done but it would take time. The sett was five galleries deep; there were far more chambers than this small group of wandering badgers would need, but many breeding seasons lay ahead of them. They would rebuild, not only the earth structure but also a declining colony, and make it a regal place for future generations.

Krag regarded his companions steadily as though seeking their approval. But they, too, showed excitement, sensing that this was their promised home to which they had returned. Already two of the boars were scratching out a hole, a show of acceptance and gratitude towards their leader.

Krag sighed his contentment as he watched them work.

Jetta's nose brushed against his own, and he knew that he had achieved a lifelong ambition and satisfied an urge which had been driving him on since he had first left this place, a cub trotting behind his parents, sad because they were leaving, not understanding why but even then promising himself that one day he would return.

Dawn came slowly, the first mist of Autumn reluctant to clear, swirling over the hills and wisping through the small wood. Gradually, the morning sunlight dispersed the grey vapour, bringing with it a warmth that was more gentle than the fierce heat of recent weeks. The badgers retired below ground, huddling in one of the upper galleries, already embarking upon a routine which they would follow in the months ahead. There were more holes to be opened up, dead leaves and bracken to be brought in for bedding. Some of the boars would hunt, others would dig. Krag would instruct them, sharing their tasks as soon as he was strong again. In such a way he commanded their respect.

Their new surroundings meant a change of diet, for rabbits and small rodents were not in abundance here. Mostly the badgers had to satisfy themselves with beechmast and roots which were in plentiful supply. Krag was puzzled about the scarcity of wildlife. Perhaps it was the drought which had driven away the smaller creatures, and when the rains came again they would return.

The October moon rose and Krag was well satisfied with the work they had done so far. They had ample, comfortable quarters for the coming Winter, and any work which was undone could be left until the Spring. There was something comforting about the prospect of the cold weather that lay ahead. They would be snug and warm in their sett, and it was a chance to rest from their labours. They had survived a troubled summer, but it had all been worthwhile.

They had earned their reward. Peace.

Chapter Twelve

Yet that tranquillity was destined to last for little more than a month, a brief respite after the badgers' travels, nothing more. With the November moon came the woodcock, those brown, long-billed birds which return, year after year, to the same wood, often to the same patch of undergrowth, their migratory instincts guiding them across sea and land from countries as far afield as Russia and Scandinavia, until they arrive at their winter home. They liked Badger Wood, as some of the locals now called it, these country folk preferring a name that was not reminiscent of Civil War atrocities. It was left undisturbed by Man and there were ample insects upon which to feed.

Krag saw the first arrival as he was foraging for food, a silent bat-like bird jinking in flight, silhouetted against the white fluffy cloud which obscured the moon, dropping out of the sky and alighting in a clearing. It stood for a moment on its tall, spindly legs, then sank down and squatted amidst the dead leaves, its colourings rendering it invisible. The woodcock was exhausted after its long flight, and now it would rest, perhaps not moving for a couple of days. Krag had no intention of disturbing it, his head upturned, watching for others which he knew would shortly follow the first one.

They came at intervals, and by the time the moon waned a dozen or more had landed in that isolated wood. In a few days some of them would move on in search of new habitat, others would remain. It was always the way.

A couple of days later a man was seen in the region of Badger Wood. Skal, one of the young boars who had been lying outside the sett, saw him and came to tell Krag. Krag immediately left the chamber and went out to see for himself, moving stealthily through the bracken until he came to a vantage point which afforded him a view of the slopes below and beyond, where he could see without being seen.

Now he saw the man. He was puzzled, for the stranger was neither farmer nor gamekeeper, carried neither stick nor gun, and wore a hat and long coat to protect him from the chill autumnal wind. He walked to and fro, pacing methodically, every so often stopping to look around him as though he was searching for something in the undergrowth. Krag remained there watching until at last this human intruder turned and began to descend the hillside, picking his way with care until he was lost from view below the brow.

Krag did not understand and that made him uneasy. Had the man carried a gun and hunted the scrub for rabbits then there would have been nothing unusual in his presence close to Badger Wood. Yet, the other had a mysterious purposefulness about him that did not liken him to a casual walker. Krag was disturbed.

The next morning some more men arrived. Krag heard the sound of an approaching vehicle and was at his lookout post long before the khaki-coloured Land Rover came into view, its heavy engine and 4-wheel drive making a mockery of the steep climb. It came to a halt barely fifty yards from the wood and three men alighted. In spite of his short-sightedness Krag had no difficulty in recognising the man who had come here yesterday. He had brought two companions with him this time, and together they unloaded some sharpened wooden stakes and heavy hammers. Then they departed in different directions with that same automaton-like walk, stopping every so often to drive a stake into the ground, the dull thudding echoing across the surrounding hills.

Their task took them most of the day, and they returned to the parked vehicle many times to fetch more stakes. It was dusk before they were finished, and they had to use their powerful headlights in order to find the track by which they had come.

That night Krag and Skal went to inspect the stakes. The wood was smooth and unnatural, gave off a sharp, unpleasant odour. The younger badger was frightened, Man was planting some new atrocity, he was sure. However, Krag was not prepared to move his colony on again merely on the strength of suspicion. They must wait and see what was going on. These men did not bring terriers or guns, and he thought that they were completely unaware of the nearby sett. Besides, it was nearly Winter, and an evacuation of the sett would mean not only finding other suitable quarters but there would be no time in which to renovate them before the snows arrived. For the moment they must remain where they were and maintain a constant vigil. At the first sign of danger, Krag promised, he would lead them elsewhere.

Skal accepted his leader's decision with a sullenness that was in itself a warning to the old badger of what would surely happen when Spring arrived. Already Skal's thoughts had turned to leadership and power, and he might well challenge for it when the buds began to show on the trees and bushes. For once, Krag hoped that it would be a long hard Winter, and he consoled himself with the thought that the leaves had not finished falling yet. There was much to do before then, and uppermost in his mind was the coming of these workmen. He wished that he had some idea of what they were planning.

The badgers kept a continual watch throughout the daylight hours, those stakes a reminder that Man would return, and when he did so it would not be without a purpose. Days passed, heavy rain fell and then turned to a thick mist which clung to the wooded hills, bringing with it a penetrating dampness which made the nocturnal foragings for food a task to be completed as quickly as possible so that the hunters could return to their warm, dry sett below ground.

A strong wind dispersed the mist eventually, and the sun shone again, its slight warmth a faint reminder of that long hot Summer which had left its mark on the landscape. With the fine weather the men returned, as though they had been lurking in the village below waiting for the low cloud to clear, arriving with startling suddenness shortly after first light. This time there were more of them, those who had driven in the stakes arriving in the Land Rover, and six others who came in three huge tractors, pulling rusty ploughs behind them.

Krag and Skal watched with growing uneasiness from the edge of Badger Wood. Lately Skal seemed unwilling to let Krag out of his sight, but now Krag welcomed the other's company. He began to wonder if he should have heeded Skal's advice and moved on elsewhere, for the presence of so many humans boded ill for the badgers. Whatever these men were planning, it would certainly not be in the best interests of the creatures of the wild.

The men crowded around the Land Rover, the tall one with the weatherproof coat spreading out a large sheet of coloured paper on the bonnet. They talked and talked, and for an hour or more it seemed that they were confused by their surroundings, for they pointed in varying directions and frequently consulted their leader. At last the paper was folded up, the three men who had come on the previous week climbed back into the vehicle, and with a shaking of their heads the remaining six turned their attention to the tractors. The powerful engines were started up and then left to tick over steadily. Another conference followed; two of them began to erect a shelter, a structure of poles over which they fastened a sheet of heavy green canvas. An empty oil drum, with holes knocked in its sides and bottom, was unloaded from one of the tractors and set up on some flat stones.

Krag and Skal eased themselves back into a thorn thicket as one of the men made his way towards the wood, treading noisily through the undergrowth, gathering an armful of dry branches.

Soon a fire was burning in the makeshift brazier, and the workmen clustered around it, warming their hands, and only standing back when the blackened kettle began to hiss and steam. They seemed more interested in eating and drinking than whatever it was they had come here to do, allowing the tractor engines to purr on unheeded. One spluttered and cut out, but they seemed not to notice, talking and laughing, obviously in no hurry to begin their day's work.

Eventually, three of them walked over to the tractors and drove off in the opposite direction, the other stoking the fire and remaining in the shelter.

Krag and Skal listened to the sounds of the tractors. They were unable to see them for they were below the brow of the hill, but the tone of the engines had changed, that fast hum had dropped to a steady, low whine. The badgers did not know why, but it puzzled them. Perhaps if they could have seen the ploughs churning up the scrubland, and turning it over into symmetrical furrows, they would have understood. But it was nightfall, long after the Land Rover had returned to take the men away, before the badgers ventured forth to explore. They sniffed at the newly-turned earth, wondered where the vegetation had gone. Skal scratched some of the soil away and burrowed down, curious to discover what lay beneath. He found some bracken, dragged it up to the surface. He had already made up his mind to challenge Krag for the leadership in the Spring but in the meantime he regarded the other as a fellow creature to be tolerated.

They returned to the sett. Skal suggested, without consulting Krag, that they should move now. Krag silenced him with snapping jaws and was relieved when his small council supported him. At least they were still on his side . . . for the time being. But he knew that their loyalty would not last beyond the end of the Winter.

Krag reminded them that they must not desert this wood except in the event of a direct onslaught by the men. So far the humans had shown little interest in Badger Wood itself except to gather kindling for their fire. They had not even appeared to notice the mounds of freshly excavated earth, nor the well-used tracks. They had no interest in the badgers. Yet, not even the wise old badger could explain what was happening. What was the purpose behind the burying of the undergrowth?

Only the jay and the magpie understood, and they did not converse with badgers except to warn them of the approach of an enemy. The sentinel magpie, who perched lower down on the wooded hillside, had watched the arrival of the workmen, and during the course of the day he had flown up into a tree directly above the tractors and observed them closely. He had seen it all before, these same ploughs destroying acres of undergrowth in Swinfen Wood to prepare for the planting of fir saplings. Now it was happening here, the destruction of established timber and scrub so that conifers could be grown, creating an alien, artificial landscape. In the Spring, he decided, he would lead his mate in search of a more remote, unspoiled wood, in which to rear their young. Life, nowadays, was a continual process of retreat. One day, perhaps not in his time, there would be nowhere left to go.

Day after day the workmen returned, and the hills rumbled to the sound of steady ploughing, an unhurried process which destroyed the landscape relentlessly. But the men were lazy, and every morning after the Land Rover had departed they sat about drinking tea for a long time before they began work.

The badgers watched and waited, each night leaving the wood to explore the fresh ploughings. Work had commenced at the furthest point from Badger Wood, but gradually it was coming closer. Now the tractors were ploughing below the badger sentry and Krag realized that the machines were heading directly towards the wood, burying brambles and pushing out gorse bushes as they progressed. But he did not wish to alarm the others, and thankfully Skal had not guessed. He would wait and see, perhaps the men would spare the wood. He would not evacuate the colony until there was no possible doubt in his mind that the old trees would be felled and the ground beneath them ploughed.

More implements were brought for the workers and stored in the canvas shelter; chainsaws that would cut through the massive trunks of century-old oaks in a matter of minutes. A man entered the wood, examined some of the largest trees, and nodded to himself. They would offer no real obstruction to the work. He returned to his companions seated around the brazier. They brewed and drank more tea and laughed as they looked towards Badger Wood. Tree-felling would make a pleasant change from continual ploughing.

At last Skal guessed what was about to happen and confronted Krag angrily for not warning them. This time the council did not support their leader when he rebuffed the young boar. Krag sighed, knew that he had to tell them the truth. He did not know why Man was destroying the landscape but it seemed the wood was destined for the same fate. Tomorrow night they would move on, abandoning their winter quarters which they had renovated. He had no idea in which direction they would go, just somewhere away from the disturbance. Perhaps there was a disused fox-earth beyond the furthest skyline. Yes, this would be their last night in Badger Wood, his own birthplace, for its days were numbered.

In the wild, the weather is the most unpredictable factor of all. Sometimes it recognizes the seasons and changes with startling suddenness; a deep fall of snow in late April, thawing the next day, or a howling blizzard in mid-November which lies on the hilltops awaiting the coming of winter.

The fine weather had enabled the forestry men to work unhindered, and but for their laziness and reluctance to begin ploughing early in the mornings, Badger Wood might have been felled a week earlier. The furrows were now barely twenty yards from its boundary, and on the morrow the air would vibrate with the harsh whine of the chainsaws, the tractors following to drag the fallen trees aside to make way for the ploughs.

The workers anticipated the change eagerly, for ploughing day after day was tedious, but when they awoke the following morning it was raining heavily and their enthusiasm waned. Their bosses, the men who sat behind desks in the warmth and comfort of a heated office, plotting the desecration of the environment from maps pinned to the walls, did not regard wet weather as an obstruction to their schedule. Snow hindered the work, but not rain.

So, as usual, the Land Rover picked up the six men in the village. It was raining steadily, and they sat without talking in the back of the vehicle as it left the hard road and commenced the steep climb over rugged ground.

Hopwas Wood lay on their left, and now the driving rain which reduced visibility had a denser texture. Sleet. Half a mile further up the hill it was snowing hard, and had been for some time because the ground ahead was an unbroken carpet of white. The wheels slipped and slid but regained their grip. The vehicle was designed for such conditions but already the driver was looking for a level stretch where he could turn round and retrace his wheeltracks which were rapidly filling in. He might have made it up to the summit, but his efforts would have been futile, for today work would be impossible.

The workers' mood of depression evaporated, they began talking and laughing. There would be no work for them up on the hills today; they would return when the thaw came, it could be tomorrow or the day after. On the other hand, the drifts might lie for weeks, frozen hard by severe overnight frosts. There was no way of telling, not even the weather forecaster knew for certain.

The badgers had sensed the advent of snow long before the first flakes began to fall, silently cloaking the hills as the night wore on. By morning the entrances to the sett were blocked and they were forced to dig their way out. They floundered to the fringe of the wood and lay watching and waiting. But there was no sign of the forestry workers and later the animals returned below ground.

Their decision to evacuate their homes was postponed. They would not relinquish it readily, and they sensed in their own way that the sudden change in weather conditions had granted them a reprieve. Life for them would continue as before until Man returned.

Chapter Thirteen

*B*aal had been unhappy for the past few weeks, ever since Reuben had turned up at Davies's farm with a young badger cub. The gamekeeper had caught it during a raid on a small sett in Hopwas Wood but his contacts in the city refused to buy it; it was too young and they could not be bothered to keep it until it was mature enough to be of use in their evil sport.

Rather than turn it loose, Reuben had offered it to Davies for whatever the farmer was prepared to pay. The two men had talked for some time in the yard, glancing in Baal's direction from time to time. Baal had a good idea what they were discussing. His greatest fear was that Davies might exchange him for the earth-pig and thus condemn him to a cruel fate. The badger regretted not having accepted his freedom when Krag had offered to help him to escape. Now it was too late.

At length Reuben and Davies reached an agreement and a five pound note exchanged hands. His children had become attached to Baal and Davies was not prepared to let him be used for badger-baiting. The cub would be a companion for

Baal, it wouldn't be any trouble because the children would feed it.

But from that moment onwards Baal was no longer the object of the children's attention. They virtually ignored him, bestowing all their affection upon the small, lovable silver-grey cub which had not yet grown its stripes. They gave it a silly name, one which at once identified it with Man – Ben. During the weeks that followed they ignored Baal, and often it was the old farmer who fed him because the youngsters either forgot or could not be bothered. On a couple of occasions Baal went hungry because Davies was busy and he, too, forgot. Usually a few scraps were thrown down in front of the kennel and seldom did the humans even bother to speak to Baal now.

Now Baal realised what captivity meant to a creature of the wild, an ignominious loss of freedom and affection. He yearned for the wooded hillsides, his old haunts, and to be able to hunt for food after dark. Yet he made no attempt to pull that rusty staple out of the wall and shamble off into the night. Up until now life at the farm had been pleasant, he had enjoyed the chattering of the children and the way they made a fuss of him. Perhaps they would tire of Ben when he grew up. They had not housed the young badger with Baal on their father's advice, fearing lest the older creature might kill the cub in a fit of jealousy. Eventually, they might kennel them together and that way, at least, Baal would have a share of the attention. He clung to that hope.

Then, one evening, when autumn was well advanced, Davies came out into the yard just after darkness had fallen. Baal was hungry, and he was disappointed to see that the farmer had not brought him any food. Davies stroked the striped head, and then those familiar gnarled fingers fumbled with the collar around Baal's neck and began to unfasten the buckle. It fell away and the badger stood there, surprised and confused, not understanding.

"Off you go, then!" There was an unaccustomed huskiness in his voice. "You're free to go, you've earned it, old feller. And just mind that Reuben doesn't get his hands on you again. He's a bad 'un!"

Baal crouched there, perplexed. He understood, all right, but after the months of captivity, freedom was suddenly a frightening prospect. The chain which had fastened him to the wall jangled loosely in the farmer's hands. They looked at each other, sadness in Davies's eyes, bewilderment and fear in Baal's. The chain fell, clinked on the stones, and Davies waved his arms the way he did when he attempted to drive his roosters into the henhouse at dusk.

"Go on, then. What are you waiting for?" He spoke gruffly. "Get off with you while you've got the chance!"

Baal backed away. His instincts urged him to run before the farmer changed his mind, but for some reason he still lingered. A heavy-booted foot kicked out at him, designed to miss, a half-hearted show of impatience.

"Get off, and don't come back hanging around here!"

The words lacked conviction, were tinged with regret, but, all the same, Baal knew that he was expected to go. He was being shown kindness in its most basic form; Davies was giving him his freedom rather than handing him back to the gamekeeper. The badger grunted, broke into an ungainly run. He paused once to look back, saw the farmer silhouetted against the lights of the house behind. The badger bore no malice towards his former captor, nor the children who had rejected him. His bitterness was directed at that pretty little earth-pig which would grow up like himself before long. In turn it, too, might find itself banished from here for the same reason. But there was no going back. This was the end. He was free.

He ambled away, crossed the narrow lane, scrambled up the grassy bank and found a gap in the hedge which led into the field beyond. The old trails were familiar even after all this time. He had not forgotten, but life was going to be much harder from now on. He must hunt for himself, no longer would his food be brought to him, and he had to rediscover that constant wariness which had once meant the difference between life and death.

He covered a short distance and then stopped to rest. He was breathing heavily and his short legs seemed scarcely able to support his bulky weight. He had lived too easily for too long, his only exercise being the constant tramping to and fro to the extent of his chain until he had finally succumbed to captivity and ceased his restless pacing. After that he had grown fat and lazy. It had not mattered whilst the children had fed and petted him, but back in the wild he was at a disadvantage. His inability to move swiftly and easily worried him, and he wondered if he would ever become Baal the aggressive young boar again.

The journey back to Hopwas Wood took him a long time, and when eventually he arrived at his destination he was weak and breathless. He doubted the wisdom in returning to his former haunts, especially since Shaf had not been to visit him for some time. Perhaps all the badgers had deserted the wood, seeking refuge elsewhere from Reuben.

Baal lay in the undergrowth bordering the wood. It was not only exhaustion which prevented him from entering this place which he knew so well, rather the fear of what he might find in there, a desolation which meant that he was totally alone, a desertion of the old sett by his own kind.

The wind rustled through the last of the dead leaves which stubbornly clung to the boughs, and thick cloud obscured the stars above. Baal scented the coming of winter, an early snowfall was imminent. A year ago he would have welcomed the change, relaxed in the snugness of the deep sett, but now it disturbed him. He was unprepared, there was no warm bed of moss and dried leaves, and pangs of hunger rumbled in his stomach. It was a long time since he had been really hungry. At the farm, especially in the early days, there had always been food there for the eating, too much of it, in fact. Now he must recapture all the old ways as quickly as possible, otherwise he would die like an abandoned pet unable to fend for itself.

He explored his old haunts, soon picking up the wide track which led to the sett, a trail which he had once helped to flatten with his constant nocturnal travellings. Something scurried away through the dead bracken at his approach. Its movements were darting, light and swift, scarcely audible above the soughing of the breeze. He recognized it as a fieldmouse, was relieved that his senses were as acute as ever but he doubted his ability to run it down and catch it. His fitness had been lost since the Spring, and now he was paying the full price for those months of inactivity. Again he regretted spurning Krag's offer to help him to escape earlier. Shaf had also tried to persuade him. Had he heeded them, by now he would have forgotten the affection once shown to him by Man and been a creature of the wild again. He was saddened, confused. And very frightened.

Baal stood looking at the sett in the clearing, his heart even heavier. It bore little resemblance to the home which he had once known. The mounds of excavated soil were higher and the entrances were gaping chasms that yawned black and seemingly bottomless. It was a desecration that had not been brought about by the claws of his own species. Man had dug down and in so doing had destroyed.

The galleries and chambers were no more, the soft soil bearing no badger spoor, and there were no fresh claw marks on the trunks of the surrounding silver-birches. Baal had returned too late, the badgers had already left Hopwas Wood and he had no idea where they had gone. Probably they had gone further up into the wooded hills, but there were hundreds of places where they might now be. He remembered the Soldiers' Wood, it was a place which he had always avoided.

Baal was very hungry. He shuffled off into the trees until he was away from the sett, and began to sniff amongst the fallen leaves. Beechmast was plentiful and he ate ravenously. The abundance of food meant that there had been no badgers here for weeks. Neither were there any grey squirrels in the vicinity, either. Everything had fled from this wood which had long been a sanctuary, and once his hunger was satisfied, Baal determined to leave also. For now Hopwas Wood was the domain of Reuben, the slayer of wildlife.

Baal headed uphill. After a short time, though, the steep climb began to take its toll of his muscles which had turned to fat during the long summer months. He was compelled to rest more frequently, and finally he took a westerly course across the face of the hills where the going was easier, travelling parallel to the village far below.

In due course he came to an area of flat ground on which grew a few stunted pines, planted in some bygone age by an unknown shepherd in an attempt to provide scant shelter for any ewe which became lost. A kindly thought, but little more than a token against the gales and drifting snows of countless winters. It offered a brief resting place for a weary badger.

Baal remained there only a short time, for he knew that before dawn he must find somewhere that offered greater safety and shelter. A long drawn out scream reached him on the wind; Tosca was in need of Rus again. She was early with her calling for a mate, but possibly she, too, sensed the early approach of winter and was letting him know her whereabouts. The sound gave him comfort, the knowledge that life in some parts of the hills went on as before. He listened intently, but there was no answering bark from the dog-fox. Rus, it seemed, was not yet ready.

The badger continued his journey, and before dawn he found a thick bed of gorse. He searched through it but there was no convenient disused fox-earth which he might have used, so he stretched himself out beneath its prickly foliage. He slept heavily. Suddenly he was awoken by a sound which had been only too familiar throughout his life amongst human beings, yet out here in the wilderness the noise gave cause for concern and wariness. The approaching engine was labouring up the steep hillside, faltering occasionally then picking up again with louder, greater determination.

Baal crawled to the edge of the gorse and peered out. Although he was handicapped by the natural short-sighted-ness of his species, his stay at the farm had increased his powers of vision in daylight. He blinked in the grey light of morning but he had no difficulty in making out the vehicle which approached and then passed by. He saw the men sitting in the rear, and continued to watch until the Land Rover was hidden from his view over the horizon. He had overslept, he should have been far from here by now. He was already paying the price of his enforced idleness.

Man, it seemed, was becoming more and more interested in places where he had seldom ventured before. Baal was perturbed, but he decided to remain where he was. There was too much open ground all around him, and if those men spotted him, he would have been easily overtaken by the vehicle had they wished to harm him. He knew that they had no dogs with them for he would surely have heard them barking. Terriers setting out on a hunt were seldom quiet, and without terriers those men would not be hunting badgers.

Shortly afterwards the Land Rover returned, and Baal followed its progress back down that steep track to the village at the bottom. This time the only occupant was the driver, and the badger wondered why the others had remained behind.

Time passed, and then the stillness was shattered by the whine of engines again, slower and more powerful ones that reminded Baal of the big red tractor which Davies used daily. Throughout the rest of that day Baal remained in the gorse thicket, the droning ceasing for a short time around midday, and then resuming until the Land Rover returned to collect the men. Only then did tranquillity return to the hills, and with it came nightfall and a freshening of the wind, the clouds darker and heavier than earlier. Baal knew that it would snow before dawn and that he must find a warmer shelter. He was hungry again, too.

He left the gorse bed and headed uphill. Once over the skyline a scent assailed his nostrils which caused him to stop and peer ahead uncertainly. The freshly turned earth reminded him of the badger-diggers and their wanton destruction. All around him, where he had expected to see an area of scrub woodland, there stretched countless furrows of ploughed earth, reminiscent of the fields around Davies's farmhouse. There he accepted it, here he could not.

Then Baal saw the wood. It seemed to hang precariously on the steep slope, old established trees that had somehow secured a roothold and clung on, defied everything that the elements had thrown at them. There was something about it, an attraction which extended an inexplicable welcome, a haven in a hostile land where the hand of Man was constantly against the inhabitants of the wild, forcing them to run. And run. Until there was nowhere left to go. Except here.

Yet between Baal and this sanctuary lay the ploughing, row after row of deep furrows, a stark reminder that the enemy of his kind had infiltrated here, too. There would be no point in establishing a winter home here, for those men would return tomorrow, and it was evident that they were already too close to this wood to offer him the peace and quiet which he sought. He had decided to head on uphill when his hunger pangs reminded him of his need for food. Beneath those trees he would surely find edible roots, perhaps even an unwary vole that would be too surprised to elude him.

Baal began to cross the furrows, his feet sinking into the soft soil and causing him to flounder, the sweet smell of the upturned landscape a constant reminder that he must be far from here by morning.

Even before Baal entered the wood he knew that badgers lived here. He sensed their presence and his wariness returned. There was no way of knowing whether they were friend or foe, whether they would offer him hospitality or chase him away. They had found this place first and it was their home. Thus, he was a trespasser and as such the resident boars might well attack him on sight.

It was a chance which he had to take if he was to eat. He changed direction, advanced on the wood upwind, circling and approaching it from the other side, moving stealthily, stopping to listen every few yards. The tracks which he followed were well-trodden but he was puzzled by the obvious disuse into which the holes which he came upon had fallen. The entrances were partially blocked by rain-washed soil and no attempt had been made to clear them. It was strange, indeed.

The sett was quite obviously a very big one, larger than any which he had seen previously. After a brief foray, which yielded a nest of hibernating beetles and some pig nuts, he scratched his way into one of the holes. The obstruction only took him a few minutes to clear and then he found himself in a large gallery. It was damp and smelled musty but, nevertheless, he was grateful for the shelter it offered from the whipping, icy wind. He would be on his way again at daylight, he decided, far from these Men who churned up the ground, and from the badgers which occupied part of this huge sett. He sensed the nearness of the animals, knew that they were somewhere in the depths of these galleries and chambers, hopefully unaware of his presence.

He dozed, and then drifted into an exhausted sleep, unaware that outside the first snow flakes were already beginning to fall.

Chapter Fourteen

Baal awoke with a feeling of uneasiness. Normally he would not have slept so long or so deeply, but this was due to a combination of exhaustion after the months of idleness and the changing of his habits in captivity. At Davies's farm, particularly in the early weeks, the children had given him little rest during the daytime so he had been forced to sleep at nights, contrary to his natural cycle, being disturbed only on those occasions when Shaf had visited him.

He knew that dawn had broken, but the daylight which filtered down to him had a stark whiteness about it which dazzled him. He moved up to the exit and saw the snow which covered the outside world, only the siting of this particular tunnel preventing the blizzard from drifting and blocking it completely.

Cautiously, he eased forward and peered outside, saw the snowflakes driving relentlessly through the trees, the leaden sky warning him that the blizzard would not be abating in the immediate future. For the time being he had no choice but to remain where he was.

The day wore on. The snowstorm eased as the wind dropped but it did not peter out altogether. There was no sign of the men who had ploughed the adjoining landscape, nor of the other badgers. This did not altogether surprise Baal for humans would not work in such conditions, and the badgers would be unlikely to show themselves before nightfall. He was still tired. It would take time for his body to adapt to the rigours of life in the wild again. Sleep seemed to be the best way of passing the daytime hours.

When Baal woke for the second time darkness had fallen. He knew that he must go above ground to search for food, burrowing down beneath the powdery snow and scratching amidst the hidden carpet of leaves in the hope of coming across beetles or small rodents. Perhaps, if he was swift, he could be back in his temporary home before the other badgers stirred. Most certainly, though, they would see his tracks and become aware of his presence.

It had stopped snowing altogether. The stars scintillated overhead in the cloudless sky, and already a severe frost had made the snow beneath him crisp and crunchy, even supporting his weight in places. It was impossible to move quietly.

After a few yards he began to dig, finding the snow soft and wet under the top frozen layer, and soon his long snout was snuffling in the dead foliage. Tonight his luck appeared to have deserted him for it was a long time before he located the first beetle. He persevered, came upon some shrews in a shallow hole, and eventually found some roots. He ate as he scratched around, relaxing only when his gnawing hunger was appeased.

Finally, he made his way back to his quarters, and as he rounded a bend behind two giant, snow-laden oak trees, their gnarled branches entwined as though attempting to shelter the rest of the wood, he found his way barred by two badgers.

He halted abruptly, backed away instinctively, and it was only then that he recognized the old boar who confronted him with bared fangs. It was Krag! The other badger was vaguely familiar, too. Skal had grown to maturity these past months, but when Baal had last seen him he was little more than a half-grown earth-pig.

Krag grunted his surprise and stepped forward, a move which prevented the aggressive Skal from launching an instant attack upon the newcomer. Skal made no attempt to disguise his displeasure at this reunion, but Krag was still leader . . . for the moment.

Krag was pleased to see Baal for their former rivalry was in the distant past and, anyway, the old badger had no longer cause to defend his position. If necessary, he would relinquish it when Spring arrived, although he doubted whether Skal's ferocity matched his wisdom. There was always the possibility that one of the other boars would make an even more determined challenge, but already the council were holding Skal in awe. And that was not a good sign.

Baal and Krag talked for a long time on the frozen snow beneath the old oaks. Baal told of his unexpected release from Davies's farm and how his wanderings had brought him to this part of the hills. Krag, in turn, related the adventures which had befallen the badgers since the summer. Reuben had been responsible for everything that had happened to them but now they faced a mightier foe, a much more impersonal one which would reduce their sett to level, ploughed earth within the space of a single day. Not even these trees, which had survived a century of gales, could withstand the invincible tide of commercial afforestation. One small wood would be destroyed, unnoticed, forgotten except by those creatures which had been rendered homeless.

Krag invited Baal to return to the main winter gallery with them, ignoring the disapproving grunts from Skal. When the thaw came they would have to move on again, and Baal would be useful in any work which might be necessary in order to renovate some disused fox-earth for the following winter. Also, Krag saw in Baal a new ally, one who might possibly become their leader, for in Skal he noted the makings of another Dul, that streak of cruelty and the desire to gain power for his own benefit. Possibly Skal had learned from their enforced stay in the Soldiers' Wood.

The other badgers made Baal welcome, and only the threat posed by the ploughs marred his homecoming. Every one of them knew that their safety was temporary, and that they could remain in Badger Wood only as long as the snow lay deep upon the surrounding hills.

Part Four:

WINTER

Chapter Fifteen

*T*he snow did not thaw with the usual rapidity of a late Autumn fall. The blizzard was followed by a succession of severe frosts, and the days of bright sunlight did no more than melt the snow on the topmost branches of the trees in Badger Wood. Autumn slipped steadily into Winter under the camouflage of a white landscape.

Still the forestry workers did not return, and for the badgers life continued normally. There was sufficient small rodent life beneath the snow and leaves to satisfy their hunger, their sharp claws digging through it with ease. One night they spied Rus on the hillside above, nose to the ground, brush trailing behind him, his every movement showing up starkly against the white background. He had scented a hare but it had eluded him on the frozen landscape. He quartered back and forth, eagerly trying to pick it up again, and at one stage Krag thought that the fox was heading for the wood. Then, barely ten yards from the outer trees, Rus turned and bounded away as if some invisible barrier had prevented him from encroaching upon badger territory. Somewhere further up in the hills, Tosca screeched.

That could have been the reason for the dog-fox's change of mind.

December arrived and with it the wind changed to a westerly direction and became warmer. The stream was transformed into a raging torrent, cascading down its rocky course, the thaw causing it to overflow its banks below Badger Wood. On the lower ground the ice on the reed-fringed pool in a corner of Davies's field melted. The mallard and teal which had deserted it earlier sensed that the water would be open again, and as the evening shadows lengthened they circled warily, hesitantly, sharp eyes searching for the slightest sign of Man before they came gliding in with guttural quacks and piping whistles. In the shallows they found ample golden barley, and such was their greed that they did not question how it came to be there. Wild duck have short memories, and they had already forgotten the barrage of gunfire which greeted their last visit here prior to the big freeze. Reuben had fed them grain, and they would continue to flight in nightly, their approach less cautious each time. Then, one evening the men from the city would once more be crouched in ambush with their guns, and Reuben would be complimented upon his work. Occasionally the game-keeper visited the pool alone, and killed some mallard which he sold to a poulterer, but his employers knew nothing of this. Only Davies heard the gunfire as he shut up his poultry for the night, but he did not say anything to anybody for Reuben could be a dangerous enemy.

A week passed and then the Land Rover returned to the workings alongside Badger Wood. The badgers saw them, but for the moment they were not unduly concerned because there were only two men. One was the tall man in the long coat who always carried a stick. He checked the tractors but made no attempt to start them. He seemed to be more concerned with poking his stick into the ground, stamping on the squelchy surface, and then shaking his head slowly from side to side.

The badgers held a meeting that night. Krag told them that he thought that the ploughing would be started again soon, but as the men appeared to show no enmity towards the animals there would be no need to evacuate the sett until the felling of the trees began. Once the saws went to work, then they would leave that same night. Skal argued that it would be better to go now and find another home before the severe weather returned, but the council supported their leader. Skal retired to a corner to sulk, and for the remainder of that night no more was heard from him.

Baal entertained them with stories of life with the humans, pointing out that there were good and bad amongst them just as there were in badger colonies. He glanced sideways at Skal and the other turned away. Davies was a good man in his own way, Baal added, whilst Reuben was evil. Nevertheless, it was Man who threatened their existence. He was still their only enemy.

It was a week before the gang of workmen returned. They seemed even more dissatisfied than before and were reluctant to begin work after the departure of their transport, sitting on felled tree trunks, drinking tea and talking. They clearly did not like working in such a remote place, much preferring the close proximity of a village where ale and company were to be found in the warmth of an inn at mid-day.

At last, though, they started up the tractors, experiencing some difficulty with one, all of them lending a hand until finally the engine stuttered and chugged into life, pumping out clouds of black, evil-smelling fumes from its exhaust.

The canvas shelter had suffered in the blizzards and two of the workers spent most of the day repairing it. Then they fetched kindling from close by the badger sett in order to keep the brazier burning. They appeared not to notice the well-used runs, nor the scoring on the bark of the surrounding trees. Their lunch break lasted until well into the afternoon, and the sun was already low in the western sky by the time they returned to their work. Very little was done at all that day, and when the man with the long waterproof coat came to collect them, they told him that the water-logged ground had made ploughing difficult. He poked his stick into the surface and nodded his head in agreement with them.

The next day it rained heavily, an unrelenting downpour from daylight to dusk, and for most of the time the men sheltered in their hut. Their programme was so far behind schedule now that they appeared to have lost all incentive to complete their task. But even with all the delays, the ploughed area was slowly extending towards Badger Wood.

Each morning they started work later, sometimes as little as an hour's ploughing was done in the afternoon. Occasionally only three or four of the six men turned up for work, for the approach of the festive season meant that routine jobs were sacrificed so that holly could be cut and sold in the city.

Then in the middle of a rare spell of fine weather, the work was abandoned. The tractors stood idle, and nobody even came to look at them. Krag was at a loss to explain this to his council, for even he was not to know that the city market was demanding more and more Christmas trees and that every available forester had been called away to the spruce thickets. There was no urgency for ground preparation and planting.

It was another unexpected reprieve for Badger Wood. Krag and his council watched and waited, knowing that time was running out for them. Sooner or later the men would resume work in an attempt to make up for lost time.

The wind blew from the north again, a sudden overnight change of direction that brought with it a flurry of snowflakes at first light. The November blizzards, now just a memory, had been a warning from Nature of the weather which she planned for the rest of the Winter. She had hurried the hibernating creatures into preparing their quarters and food stores, whilst Krag and his badgers had chosen to make a last stand. An intervening spell of mild weather now could signal the beginning of the end for their sett. Their stubbornness might have resulted in homelessness during the severest of conditions. It was a chance that Krag took, and as the blizzards swirled in again he hoped that there would be no thaw in the coming weeks. Only the hardest of Winters would ensure their survival until Spring.

Skal was unusually quiet. No longer did he openly oppose Krag's decisions, but preferred to remain sulking in the background. He, too, was waiting. The moment those chainsaws began whining out their destruction of the habitat, he would denounce Krag for lack of foresight and make his challenge for the leadership. Then he would take the badgers to safety. He knew not where, but he would take them somewhere.

There was only one doubt in his scheming mind. Baal! The newcomer was constantly at the old boar's side, staking his own claim for when the Spring arrived. Only the destruction of Badger Wood would help Skal, and he was convinced that once the badgers were homeless he could sway the council over on to his side.

Day after day he sniffed the sharp, frosty air, anxious to scent a warm south-westerly wind that would melt the snow.

Chapter Sixteen

The snow lay deep over the hills, massive drifts building up in the open spaces. The silent tractors were little more than indistinguishable white shapes that blended with their surroundings, no different from the many jutting outcrops of rock. The canvas shelter had collapsed again under the weight of the snow, burying the brazier.

Food was scarce for the creatures of the wild but the occupants of Badger Wood were fortunate because their numbers were few and there were sufficient roots and small rodents beneath the snow to feed them. In the days of Krag's father, when every gallery in the sett was in use and there were ten times as many mouths to feed, such severe conditions would have presented a threat to their livelihood. Now it was their saviour, keeping Man at bay. But for how much longer?

The New Year came but to the badgers one day was much the same as another. Only the weather and the seasons denoted the passing of time. The creatures lapsed into a kind of semi-hibernation, enjoying the atmosphere of their deep gallery and going above ground only to hunt.

It was one of the longest and hardest Winters on record.

The Hunt was unable to ride through the deep snows, and Rus became bolder than ever in his raiding. He was even more cunning now, and had learned to outwit Reuben by plundering the game reserves on moonlit nights when the snares set in gaps in hedges and fences reflected the silvery light and warned him of their presence.

Farmer Davies shut up his poultry each dusk, checked to see that none of the birds had roosted outside. For a time both Pyne and Rus were foiled, but then Rus learned that by sneaking down in broad daylight, and making full use of the cover offered by the orchard, he could easily approach the unsuspecting hens, seize one and be away before the farmer arrived on the scene to see what was causing the frenzied clucking.

Pyne had watched his rival's success in this way on more than one occasion; so he adopted the same tactics, only for him it was much easier because he could make his way towards his intended prey through the branches of the apple trees. Frustrated at having lost six of his barnyarders in one week, Davies sent for Reuben.

Both Rus and Pyne watched Reuben setting out for the farm in his van and, unknown to each other, they made straight for that part of the Home Covert where the game-keeper fed his birds daily. Separately, they watched the pheasants greedily devouring the scattered maize, Rus crouching beneath a thorn bush, Pyne lying at full stretch on the overhanging bough of a spreading larch.

The birds scratched busily in the snow, the magnificent plumage of the cock pheasants glowing in the morning sunlight, the hens somewhat insignificant amongst them. Like the mallard at the flight pond, their greed was their undoing.

Rus sprang first, his jaws closing over the head of the nearest cock pheasant, its wings flapping frantically in his face. There was a sudden rush of wings as every bird in that clearing became airborne, the cackling of the cocks echoing down the valley as far as Davies's farm. Most of them struck out for the open fields but a few, those with full crops, decided that safety lay in the trees immediately above them. Pyne, who was on the point of venting his anger on his rival directly below him, using that obnoxious fluid with which Nature had provided him for such a purpose, changed his mind when a cock, equally as splendid as the one flapping in Rus's mouth, alighted almost on top of him.

Pyne sprang, caught his prey and tumbled to the ground with it struggling between his teeth. Fox and polecat regarded each other over their respective catches which lay twitching at their feet, and then, knowing that the alarm was raised, took off in the opposite direction to devour their breakfast at their leisure.

Reuben had barely alighted from his van in Davies's yard when he heard the 'karrup-karrup-karrup' from the Home Covert. Seconds later he was driving recklessly back down the narrow, twisting, snow-packed lanes, but by the time he reached the clearing in the wood there was not a pheasant to be seen. His worst fears were confirmed as he examined two piles of feathers, only a few feet apart. His experienced eye noted the footprints in the snow and he had no doubt concerning the identity of the culprits.

He swore vengeance on Rus and Pyne, and determined to set even more snares and traps. He remembered, too, the old badger which had eluded him in Hopwas Wood and inflicted those terrible scars on Warrior. Perhaps one morning he would find Krag caught in one of his snares. That would be an added bonus, indeed.

Chapter Seventeen

*T*owards the end of January, Nature finally decided that she had more than vented her wrath on the countryside. She possibly even regretted having allowed the severe conditions to prevail for so long and, as if in repentance, she withdrew the arctic weather with a suddenness that plunged the whole area into unprecedented floods. The course of the old stream was lost in the torrent that flooded parts of Hopwas Wood and the Soldiers' Wood, down into the river meadows below the village so that mallard, teal and wigeon were to be seen dabbling in the water-logged fields.

Badger Wood suffered less than the lower woodlands because of its elevated position, but melted snow flooded the lower galleries of the huge sett so that the badgers were forced to move in the upper chambers. The tractors were once again revealed in their stark ugliness, resurrecting the threat to the neighbouring wildlife.

There was now warmth in the sun's rays, and it set about its task of drying out the landscape. Soon the forestry workers would return to complete their destruction, and this time they would not be able to find numerous excuses for long periods of idleness.

It was a fortnight, though, before the Land Rover returned, the man in the long coat testing the ground with his stick and nodding his confirmation that it was suitable for ploughing. The watching Skal was secretly pleased. Not only was the end in sight for Badger Wood, he decided, but also for Krag and Baal.

The ploughing started again, and at nightfall Krag knew that without any doubt the men would begin felling Badger Wood on the morrow. The nearest furrow was no more than ten yards away. He called a meeting of the council that night. Skal, who had adopted a sullen silence for weeks at these gatherings, was his former aggressive self once more. No longer did he skulk in the shadows, but instead he mingled with the council boars, and demanded that the sett was evacuated this very minute without further discussion. Krag ordered him to be silent and, to the surprise of those present, Skal obeyed. His plan was working for, when they were finally forced into retreat, he would remind them of his warning. Winter was not over yet, another spell of severe weather was still possible. They should have left in the Autumn when there would have been time to find and prepare new quarters. Now they would be homeless, hungry, but Skal was prepared to endure hardships in his quest for power. That was when he would make his challenge for the leadership, with Krag and Baal at a disadvantage. Their supporters would have lost faith in them and would look to a new leader in a crisis. Skal would insist that they be banished from the colony. There might even be no need for him to contest the issue with fang and claw.

In the meantime, they agreed to wait until the whine of chainsaw was heard in the wood above, every last moment here was precious to them. They would not finally concede their home until its destruction had begun. They would escape easily because there would be no gauntlet of guns or dogs to run. The foresters did not wish to harm the badgers, all they wanted was their domain for some purpose incomprehensible to the creatures themselves.

But, miraculously, the tree felling was postponed yet again. It was as if the workmen were putting off a task which they did not relish for as long as they could, finding other chores, anything except the clearance of Badger Wood. They tinkered with the tractors, filed the teeth of their saws, ate and drank in the canvas hut. The Land Rover came for them in the late afternoon and still not a tree in Badger Wood had been harmed.

On the following morning only two of the men arrived for work, one spending most of his time in the shelter, the other continuing the maintenance of the tractors. But still Krag delayed his decision to take the badgers elsewhere for this was his own birthplace and he would only leave when there was nothing to remain here for.

Two more days passed. On the second day no men came at all. Skal was agitated; perhaps the foresters had reclaimed as much land as they needed and the wood was destined to be spared, after all. In which case, he would challenge Krag for the leadership, anyway. Krag, too, was uneasy; if their home was destined for destruction, far rather it was done now. The constant tension was becoming unbearable. What were hours, days, weeks even, in the lifespan of a mature wood?

His worst fears were confirmed on the following morning when the Land Rover arrived with the full workforce. Today they wasted no time, made straightaway for the tractors and within a quarter of an hour the ploughs were churning up the remaining scrubland, turning it over and burying the undergrowth in a continuation of the existing long, straight furrows. At each turn the heavy wheels brushed the bracken on the edge of the wood.

Three of the men were busy with the chainsaws again, fuelling and oiling them, testing the motors so that pungent diesel fumes permeated the sett, an odour of finality filling the chambers and galleries as if to hasten the occupants into the evacuation which they had delayed so long.

Krag turned to Jetta, saw the sadness in her eyes. If there had only been the two of them perhaps they would have stayed, refused to surrender their birthright and claimed their heritage for their burial ground, their bones remaining below ground for centuries, their spirits hunting the desecrated landscape in defiance of Man. But they knew that they could not commit the others to share such a fate. They had a duty to fight for the survival of the colony.

Krag eased his way up the tunnel that led to the surface, his movements slow and cumbersome, an unwillingness to accept defeat manifesting itself in a burning around his middle as though the snare that encircled him was tightening still further. He stopped once, knew that the others had halted behind him. There was no nudging, no impatient snouts urging him forward. Only Skal was pleased and he dared not show his feelings yet. There would be plenty of time for that later.

The tractors were close. Very close. The animals felt the earth vibrating, smelled diesel again. Krag poked his head out of the entrance, braced himself for the sudden rush out into the open, a scampering line of badgers that would flee uphill and over the skyline. Even now he was instinctively holding back, delaying the awful decision to abandon their home. Even these last few seconds were precious to him. Behind him one of the others grunted. He thought it was Skal.

Krag could see the tractors now, detected an urgency about them that had not been there previously, mighty machines that devoured the soil with an insatiable hunger. Three of the workmen were walking towards the wood carrying chainsaws. This time there would be no reprieve.

The badger leader was poised to run but again he hesitated.

Some strange instinct commanded him to stay just another second or two, had him staring fixedly at the nearest tractor. It was turning over the surface methodically, its engine a sinister hum, coming closer. And closer. Then, suddenly, it lurched unevenly, its agonised scream of tortured metal filling the air and causing Krag to push back against those crowding him. The plough grated, screeched again, came to a standstill as the engine was switched off. The other two tractors ground to a halt, idled, then whined to a silence.

The drivers clambered out of their cabs, clustered around the leading tractor. The men with the chainsaws were coming across to join them. Everybody had stopped work, their attention focused on that plough which was jutting up off the surface. They knelt to examine it, shook their heads, muttered to one another. Then one of them fetched a stick, began poking at the area of uncultivated ground which was now little more than a narrow strip. They shrugged their shoulders as they walked dejectedly back to their canvas shelter. The brazier was lighted and the kettle was suspended over the licking flames. After a few minutes it boiled, hissing loudly, and the men sat around drinking tea and eating their sandwiches.

Still Krag waited. He did not understand, all he knew was that for the moment the felling of Badger Wood had been postponed yet again. He dared not hope for more than a brief respite. Skal was urging the others to leave but, like the leaders, they ignored him.

The men did not resume work after their lunch. They remained in the shelter, and towards late afternoon one of them walked to the brow of the hill and stood looking for the Land Rover which arrived each evening to transport them home. Whilst the watching badgers yearned to remain here, it seemed that the forestry workers were eager to be away.

The sun dipped below the horizon and at last they heard

the approaching vehicle. For some reason it was later than usual today. The man in the long coat was clearly angry as he stalked across to where the tractors stood silent, the other watching as he probed the ground with his long stick. He used both hands, leaning on it with his full weight until it bowed and threatened to snap. He was muttering to himself as he tried other places but always with the same result, the tip refusing to penetrate deeper than a few inches. Finally, he turned away and stalked back towards the cluster of workmen.

They gathered around the Land Rover as he spread that coloured sheet of paper over the bonnet, all of them poring over it. From time to time he turned and pointed in the direction of Badger Wood, then beyond it, talking loudly. His companions either nodded or shook their heads, agreeing and disagreeing with him, but all the time impatient to be on their way home.

Baal pushed his way alongside Krag, stretched out. Neither of them understood what was happening, only that something had halted the sweeping tide of destruction. But for how long? Krag knew from his experience that Man did not give up easily. Usually he found a way to overcome problems with his massive machinery.

The badgers watched as the men climbed into the Land Rover and drove away, the tractors remaining behind as a stark reminder that the workforce would be returning. Krag scarcely dared to hope but clearly they had been granted yet another night in the old sett. The others sensed his reluctant jubilation. Only Skal remained sullen for his plans had received a setback. He told himself that it was only temporary. There was still time.

Another day dawned but it was late morning before the workers returned. With them was the one whose main interest seemed to be attempting to push his stick into the ground and another, shorter man, whom the badgers had not seen previously. The latter was-thick set, puffed out his cheeks when he talked. His checked trousers were tucked into wellington boots and he wore a dark green thorn-proof jacket with a corduroy collar. He had an air of authority about him, and even the tall man appeared to be in awe of him as together they walked across the remaining strip of unploughed land. They both poked at the surface with sticks, muttering to each other the whole time. They were clearly displeased with their findings. Then they stood with their backs towards the workmen and conversed in low tones, shaking their heads.

Finally, they returned to the Land Rover and the much-creased map was again unfolded. There was more talking and pointing, and their attention seemed to be focused on the ground beyond the wood. The workers kept their distance, awaiting the decision of their superiors.

At last the map was folded up. The tall man issued some instructions to the others, then clambered back into the Land Rover alongside his stout companion and the driver. Once their bosses were out of sight below the brow of the hill, the workers concentrated on brewing tea. To the watching badgers they seemed more relaxed than they had been recently, which was disconcerting because it meant that the foresters had found a way to overcome the problem.

The tractors were started up again. Krag and Baal watched apprehensively as the machines surged forward, ploughs raised off the ground, sweeping round in a wide circle which took them up above the wood. Here the ploughs were low-ered, began churning up bracken and grass, cutting deep as they forged out those only too familiar furrows again. In the meantime the other three workers began taking down their shelter and re-siting it on the opposite side of Badger Wood.

An extensive stretch of the upper ground had been ploughed by the time the transport vehicle returned. The men had laboured with a zest in contrast to those previous days of laziness. There was no sign of the fat man, only the tall one came and stalked around the upper perimeter of the wood, prodding the surface with his long staff. He stood and surveyed the newly-turned area, smiling his relief and satisfaction. Whatever the problem had been, they had overcome it.

Only Skal was relaxed, keeping apart from the others, unable now to disguise his smugness. None of the badgers understood what was happening, only that the attack on their domain was being launched from a different direction. The tractors had to clear and plough this area first which, at the most, would give the animals a further few days grace.

Now Skal took to voicing his warning, telling his companions that their habitat was being surrounded by a sea of new-turned earth, and that unless they fled now their escape route would be cut off; there would be no cover through which to flee, they would be seen easily. He added that these men might return with terriers, and the badgers would be unable to outrun them on the soft ground. But none heeded him. His predictions of doom were met with angry grunts, and throughout all this time the weather showed no sign of a return to Winter. If anything, there was a hint of an early Spring, an increasing warmth in the sun's rays, and Skal sensed that his cunning bid for the leadership was destined to fail.

Just as Autumn had slipped unnoticed into Winter, so Winter merged into Spring. The gradual change was only apparent to those who knew the signs, the farmers and foresters and, of course, the birds and beasts of the countryside. No longer did Tosca scream for Rus, for he had long ago answered her call, and now she was content in the depths of the earth which he had found for her, awaiting the birth of her litter. Rus hunted the hills where there were ample rabbits for the taking, and the snares which Reuben set for him lower down remained untouched.

The foresters were absent again. One afternoon they drove the tractors away behind the Land Rover, only that flimsy shelter remaining as a guarantee of their return. The badgers waited uneasily, their stronghold now an island surrounded by a sea of ploughed earth, the furrows motionless waves on a tide that neither ebbed nor flowed. But there was still the nagging fear that their sett might soon become submerged.

Krag knew that this was no time to relinquish his leadership for the badgers might still have need of his experience in matters concerning Man. Baal seemed to realize this, too, perhaps hoping to achieve a bloodless conquest in more peaceful times.

Skal, though, had returned to lurking in the background, slyly watching the other two badgers, seldom letting them out of his sight. This was a time of waiting for him, too, but his ambitions were slowly slipping away from him. If the leadership was denied him, he vowed he would take his revenge upon those who had thwarted him.

Chapter Eighteen

March arrived and starkly revealed that barren wasteland upon the hillside, a stretch of brown in contrast to the rolling greenery, Badger Wood the only reminder that once trees and scrubland had existed there. The bare artificial landscape was ugly to behold.

Nevertheless, the acres of ploughed ground held an attraction for other species of wildlife. The rabbits and hares liked to play and scratch in the powdery earth, and for the rooks and plovers a new supply of food, in the form of wire-worm, had been exposed to them by the plough. There were also those who seemed not to notice; Sacko and Pyne did not mind where they found rabbits as long as they found them, and the ever-searching sparrowhawk seemed unaware that anything had changed.

Already it was time for the badgers to breed again, and with the beginning of a new cycle they instinctively looked for a new leader, knowing that Krag's days were over. Baal made a token challenge, a low growl and a step forward, and for the first time in his life Krag turned away without retaliation.

Baal faced the council, waiting to see if there were any

other contenders. His eyes searched the darkest corner of the chamber and met the baleful stare of Skal. Skal eased forward, but the sudden rush which Baal was expecting never materialised.

Skal turned away and shambled through the nearest exist, leaving Badger Wood and crossing the ploughed ground until he disappeared from view over the distant skyline. Fate, and his own ambitions, had cast him into the role of a 'rogue' badger. From now on he was a loner, a creature which would raid the game preserves in search of easy prey, and one day, if his sly cunning deserted him, he might find himself caught in one of Reuben's fox-snares.

The change of leadership in the sett passed almost unnoticed. But whilst the sows were preparing their breeding chambers, the Land Rover and tractors brought the forestry men back up to the high ground. Their arrival was not unexpected. When the badgers heard the approaching vehicles, the vibrations reached the sett long before the cavalcade came into sight; Baal and Krag went up to the surface to watch. This time, though, Krag lay silently behind his companion. If the younger badger wanted his advice he would ask for it, otherwise Krag was just another member of the colony, and his role was to obey the new leader.

This time the tractors towed long trailers, stacked with bundles of spruce saplings scarcely a foot high. There was no sign of the man who spent much of his time prodding the ground with a stick. The watching badgers were curious but no longer concerned. Without ploughs and chainsaws, Man would not be able to desecrate their wood.

Work began on the lower side of Badger Wood, the tractors following the furrows, one man dropping the young trees off at intervals, another following behind on foot and burying the roots with a spade so that the trees stood upright. The conifers were planted close together in order to afford one another protection from the lashing gales as they grew to maturity. Only when they were strong trees would they be thinned out, those removed being used for fencing posts or pit-props. The hillside was being utilised by Man, and the wildlife was left to adapt to the change. Some would disappear, like the pheasant and the woodcock, others would remain. The badgers had chosen to stay, left undisturbed in their sett once the tree-planting was completed, only their surroundings taking on a different appearance.

Neither Baal nor Krag knew why Badger Wood had not been cut down and the ground ploughed to make way for the artificial fir forests. It was beyond their understanding that their domain rested upon a bed of *slate* and that the forestry ploughing had screeched its protests when it came into contact with the hard surface. There was nothing to be gained by felling those trees once it was discovered that the only small area of soft earth was that in which the sett itself had been excavated by the badgers decades ago.

So Badger Wood received a final reprieve and became an island amidst those symmetrically-planted conifers. By the time the earth-pigs were born the planting was completed and the workers had departed, taking even their canvas shelter with them. It would be a long time before Man returned, and that part of the hills would be left in peace.

Krag and Jetta felt more secure than ever before. They knew that the fir saplings would grow rapidly, forming an impenetrable barrier around the sett, far more effective against badger-diggers than ever the rhododendrons in Hopwas Wood had been. Only wildlife would be able to pass beneath the low, entwining branches.

Krag had achieved his ambition and returned to his birthplace, bringing Jetta and the rest of the Hopwas colony with him. He had relinquished the leadership with dignity, and from now on the responsibility was Baal's. It was the beginning of a new era, and Badger Island would survive for many generations to come, long after the battles of Hopwas Wood and the Soldiers' Wood, and the fierce drought of that terrible summer, had been forgotten.